Godalming Tales

Tales From a Couch in the Kings Arms

The Godalming Writers Group

3rd Edition 2019

ISBN:9781794214743
ISBN-13:

DEDICATION

For the residents of, and our own hometown of
Godalming nestled in the leafy suburbs of Surrey.

…and to all those writers, wherever they may be, trying to
make a start; keep trying, your day will come.

CONTENTS

ACKNOWLEDGEMENTS

All the family and friends who have supported the project

Introduction

The Godalming Writers Group met for the first time in July, 2015. Formed by a few like-minded people who, knowing that writing is a lonely business, met to discuss their passion for it. This event was as much social as it was educational.

We were all in different stages in our writing careers. Some were just starting out, with long forgotten first drafts in bottom drawers, or new writers with a passion and a need to express themselves.

At first we came together to learn, to discuss and to laugh at our common mistakes and share the loneliness of writing. We discussed the pain of a blank page that stares back, sitting in front of the screen waiting for the words to tumble forth and how to create the masterpiece that we all know we have inside us.

For some it gave us a belief to continue writing – our efforts would be rewarded (in some way).

However, soon our endeavours changed. We wanted to create something together. To put a book up on the bookshelves. To gain that which we were all craving – to be published. But what? How?

The inspiration came from the town around us. It had brought us together so we decided that Godalming would become the backdrop of our stories. A collection of stories with Godalming at its heart.

With ebbs and flows over the course of the year, we finally produced this book that you now hold in your hands. This book was made through the creativity and dedication of the Godalming's Writers Group.

We hope that you enjoy this body of work set in and about the town that brought us all together.

A town it seems, that has many stories waiting to be told.

Godalming Writers Group

https://www.facebook.com/GodalmingWritersGroup/

February 2017

ELECTRIC LIGHT – THE UNTOLD STORY

By Stefan Kuegler

Godalming in Old Picture Postcards
© Godalming Museum

A black and white image was printed in The Graphic on the 21st November 1881. They reported that Godalming was the first town in England to substitute the electric light instead of gas for lighting its public streets. However no mention was made of the public electricity supply to houses.

The man stretched.

"Carry your bags, mister?"

The man looked around, seeing a dirty boy waiting patiently - an eager look on his face.

"No, I have only one. I can manage. Where can I find a place to lay my head?"

The boy held his chin as if considering the options. "King's Arms is the one you want."

"And where would that be?"

"Down the High Street."

The man nodded picked up his bag and moved off in the direction of the town, or at least what he could see.

"Why the hell did I come here?" The man reached into his pocket for the request from his boss. He read it again to be sure that he was in the right place. He looked behind him to see if he could see anything that might indicate that he was in the wrong place.

Godalming.

He saw the sign and stopped for a moment as more of the town came into view. There wasn't much of it. Horses moved slowly along the main street – most likely this High Street. He could see nothing high about it.

"Electric light, here?"

"Yes, here."

The man turned around.

"Mr Richard Pullman, sir. And you are?" Mr Pullman held out his hand.

The man paused for a moment before reaching out his own hand and shaking Mr Pullman's most heartedly. "Miles Chester. Journalist."

"Oh, you must be here for the marvelous event. It is tomorrow you know."

"Yes, so I heard."

"Yes, can't tell you how proud we are here in Godalming. This will put us on the map, that's for sure. Great event for the town. Oh yes, great event." Mr Pullman puffed up his chest, visibly proud of his little community.

"Indeed."

Mr Pullman waited, happy and expectantly. He was obviously expecting more questions asked of him.

"And how are you involved, sir?" Miles belatedly realized that he hadn't expected to meet someone and had not prepared anything. He hadn't known what to expect. Here was a man obviously wanting to talk about the light and the town. Bursting to talk about it.

"Very proud, I am, to be involved. It is my brother and me. We, my brother and me that is, are going to have our Mills lit by the electric light. Make us famous for sure." Mr Pullman said with such reverence, as if it was something magical.

"Oh I see." He waited to see if some more was forthcoming. He wasn't ready for this. The train trip was tiring and he just wanted to get a drink.

"I'll be there tomorrow, oh yes." Mr Pullman a little lost for words but still wanting to say something. He didn't get to talk to the press often. He thought they would more interested and frankly, interesting.

"Perhaps I could have a chat with you then. Get your thoughts on the matter when it happens."

"Of course. I will be there to witness this. Oh yes, a great day for Godalming." Mr Pullman strolled away, seeming impressed with the day and the promise of the future.

Miles walked down the road, trying to stay out of the way of the horses and carriages. He looked up and down the street. It was a quaint little village. There was an odd little building, pink or something. Strange shape. Middle of the road. Not sure why they hadn't pulled it down. He wondered what it was.

He looked across the road and saw the crowd that had

gathered. He tried to see what the fuss was about and couldn't see what they were looking at until he saw one of the crowd pointing upwards. At first Miles lifted his head slightly to peer above the level of the buildings but then realised that the man had been pointing at the post with the glass bowl hanging down.

"So this was it." Miles whispered to himself. He stood for a moment, caught up in the excitement of the crowd as they all wanted touch or see the light up close. There was nothing to see since it was in the middle of the day. Miles studied the light for a moment, a tall post made of iron. It was hollow from the sound it. People were touching it and banging on it as if touching made it more real. The top of the post had a glass bowl and a metal plate which covered it. Miles knew that it was there was for reflecting the light.

He stood for a while, captivated like everyone else, expecting something. There was nothing. The post continued to stand still despite having the adoring public awaiting something special.

Miles watched for a second more and then continued to move in the direction of the public house. He hoped with all the excitement in town they had a spare bed for the night. He moved on down the street. He was happy to see the sign for the Kings Arms come into view.

Miles looked at the inn, or hotel, he wasn't sure what. It looked in good shape, majestic and inviting. He moved between the pillars into the hotel and followed the hallways around to the bar area. He stood for a while, inspecting the place as if he were to purchase it. After a nod to himself, he moved forward to the bar.

"Yes, sir?" The publican, a stout man called Ben, spoke as he moved opposite Miles. He was dressed as would any barkeep, white shirt, vest and trousers – all had seen better days - he wiped his hands on a fairly clean towel as he looked Miles up and down.

"A bed and a drink."

"In which order, sir?"

"If there is no shortage of beds then the drink first, I'm parched."

"No problem with the room, Sir. What will you have?"

"Ale."

"Certainly, Sir. And what brings to our fine town, sir?" The bartender asked as he poured the man his drink. "As if I didn't know."

"Oh?"

"You're here for the show, ain't you?"

"Show?" Miles acted dumb, in actual fact he didn't know what the man was talking about.

"The switch on."

"Of course. Yes, I am in town because of that."

"I can't place your accent. Are you from up North?"

Miles put his drink down, smiled and nodded. "Are there more people expected?"

The man behind the bar shrugged. "I'm sure the Mayor invited others but the likes of me don't know. The town is certainly agog."

"Why here?"

"Why here what, sir?"

"Why Godamningling?"

"Godalming, Sir. Who's to say? Some of the locals were taken with the thought. Nearly bewitched them it did. They wanted it so much. Wanted to put the town on the map. And by God, if they don't just do that. The name of Godalming will go down in history."

"I'm sure." Miles sighed, leaned back on the bar, surveying the people in the bar. There were a few but it was early so the real crowd would arrive later. Miles didn't mind that it would allow him some time to get changed. He had work to do and he best try to get it done early.

Miles took another long pull from his ale and motioned the bartender over.

"I'd like to see my room now."

"Of course, Sir. Just this way." The man moved down the length of the bar until he could exit it and then indicated that Miles should follow him.

"Just the one night is it, Sir?"

"Most likely."

"Of course." The bartender tried to keep the disappointment out of his voice. "It will be two shillings for the night."

Miles counted out two coins.

"That also included dinner and a few drinks for the night, Sir. Follow me." Ben moved up the stairs. He didn't look back, assuming that Miles would follow behind. After a brief walk down the hall, Ben opened a door to indicate Miles' room.

"Would this suit you?" Ben stood aside to let Miles into the room. Miles moved into the room, looking around it as he did so. It was like any of a number of rooms he had been in the past. Ben held out the key, which Miles grabbed as he stood for a moment.

"Fine, fine."

"Dinner at 6. Is there anything else?"

"No, I'm fine." Miles placed his leather bag on the bed as the door was closed. He moved to the window and saw that it overlooked the coach and stable area behind the hotel. It was empty at the moment, but Miles was sure that come evening time there would be one or two horses stabled there for coaching travelers.

Miles opened his bag and stared at the contents of it. He took a deep breath. He placed the items he would need on the bed and checked them once again. He hoped he would not need anything else. All needed now was time. He would have to wait. He would go down to the bar for his meal and then it would be time.

Miles went over the plan one more time in his head. It wasn't anything difficult but he needed to be careful. He wiped his hands over his face. He was a little tired from the trip. He could do with a little rest and freshen up and then he would be better off. He had much to learn and organize.

He looked to the sideboard and saw a jug and wash basin. He poured out some water and first washed his face. The coolness of the water revived him somewhat. He then washed his arms and neck. He used the towel next to the basin to dry himself down. He felt better and stretched out on the bed. A few minutes of sleep would help.

Miles roused himself a little later. A quick look out the window, told him that evening had fallen but it was not yet too late. He pulled himself out of bed, checked that everything was still where he left it. He pocketed the key and then moved towards the door to go to the dining area.

The smells of the cooking from the kitchen and oil based lights greeted him. It wasn't unpleasant. The noise from the bar area was louder than when he had entered previously. There were, maybe, twenty people at the bar, all in various staged of drunkenness and dress. Farmers and labourers and the like mixed as they consumed their beverage of choice, arguing the finer points of the day.

"Ready for dinner, Sir?" Ben greeted him as he entered. Miles just nodded. Ben directed him to a seat.

"Roast tonight, Sir. Being a special occasion and all."

"Oh yes."

"Would you want the usual with the roast?"

"What is the meat?"

"Pork, Sir."

"Yes."

"Right you are then, sir. Another ale?"

"Yes." Miles sat back and waited for his food and drink to arrive. Both arrived quickly and he set to. The meal was filling even if it was a little flavourless. He was seated at the end and that was the main thing. It had been a tiring day.

Even though he had ignored conversation during the course of his meal, preferring to keep his own company, he listened to the talk of the other guests. Excitement for tomorrow's event was building but there seemed to be a genuine lack of knowledge of what it all meant. The town's folk or those in the bar at least wondered what it all meant. Few had a great understanding of electricity or even how it came about. Miles had to cover his mouth a few times to stop himself laughing as he heard various patrons trying to explain it.

Miles smirked to himself. The same thoughts as before passed through his head. He felt like his mind was finally made up. The comments of the locals had confirmed what he thought but he had been willing to change his mind if he had seen something worthy of it.

He nodded to the barkeep and got up. The night was young and now there was work to do. He went back to his room and knowing that he was ready for the night. He didn't know how long it would take but he wouldn't have long.

Miles entered his room and locked the door behind him. He lit a candle to give himself some light and placed in on the one table in the room. He checked his tools one more time, making sure everything was ready.

He looked out the window from his room. He had been happy with it because it overlooked the courtyard out the back. From first glance it also seemed to have a way down from the room to the courtyard.

An exit he planned to use later tonight.

Miles lay on the bed, but sleep didn't come. The sounds of the hotel quietened down and he felt like the time had come to act. He stood and went to his door, he opened it and peered out in the corridor.

Nothing and no one.

Miles re-closed the door and locked it again, grabbed his tools. He went to the window and slowly, but not quietly, slid it open. Once he had it open enough to be able to slide out, he waited a moment to see if anyone had heard him. The hotel was still quiet.

Miles quickly made his way to the courtyard. He then stole around the front of the hotel through the carriage way.

He scanned the area but there was little to see. The oil-based lights that illuminated the courtyard showed little. The gloomy light was enough to see by but little else.

If there was something else on the streets then Miles couldn't see it.

He waited a moment more and then moved out of his hiding spot. He had an objective and he knew that the sooner he got there the quicker it would be over. He moved down the street. The object of his mission was further down the street. He had looked at it earlier and now in the dark he could see it appear like some lone tree standing in the gloom. A hall-bearer of things to come. The future.

The electric light was now in front of Miles. He looked around. The town seemed deserted.

"How could this be the future? This back-water of a place."

Miles reached around behind him, extracting the item he had secreted on himself earlier in his room.

"Good evening, sir."

Miles spun around at the voice. He dropped what he had been taking from behind his back.

"What have we here then?"

Miles moved quickly to pick it up but the shadowy man was quicker. The man straightened.

"And what were you planning on doing with this, sir?" The man held up the hammer.

"Nothing."

The man revealed himself to be a policeman. He looked at the hammer and then back at Miles. "Nothing?" The policeman spoke in a restrained manner. Acting dumb but being anything but.

"Just out for a walk with your hammer, were you, Sir? A spot of maintenance along the way? A spot of robbery?"

For a moment Miles thought he might be able to bluff his way out this spot of bother. He considered his responses as the policeman waited, waving the hammer in front of his face.

"What's going on?" A third figure strode into view.

"I was just trying to get to the bottom of it, sir. Oh, good evenin', Mr Pullman."

"Evenin', George."

Mr Pullman moved to stand beside George. "Well?" He looked at both George and Miles, expecting one of them to give him an answer.

"Can you explain why you were walking around with a hammer? Carpenter, are you?" George directed the question at Miles.

"NO," Miles was frustrated, he sighed to regain control, "I was just out for a walk." He wondered whether he could run. He felt that both men were not the fittest and he could easily lose them in the low light. His eyes darted around looking for a likely spot to hide.

"Missing something, are we?"

"Who are you?" Mr Pullman asked. "What are you trying to do?"

George moved in front of Miles, blocking some of his exits. With Mr Pullman standing at the other side, it was unlikely that he was going to be able to run between them. With the building at his back, he was cornered.

"Destroy your light." Miles snarled.

"Why? I don't understand."

"I come from New York. We are going to have the first electric light to shine in all but a week. It should be New York that is the first city. A city of importance. What are you? A back-water village that no one has ever heard of. It should be New York which is first."

"I see. Sabotage, is it?" George starred at the hammer for a moment. He could see Mr Pullman starting to get angry.

11

"If you like." Miles shrugged, not worried about the fate he would face.

"Time to cool off in the jail for the night. After tomorrow it won't matter." George grabbed Miles by the shoulder.

Mr Pullman shook his head. "I knew you weren't a journalist. Didn't ask enough questions."

"Never said I was." Miles called over his shoulder as George led him away. "What did I care about what you said. It should be New York!"

Mr Pullman stood, proud for a moment and looked up at the light. Tomorrow was going to be a special day. Tomorrow Godalming, a town mentioned in the Doomsday book and made a Royal Borough by Queen Elizabeth, would be famous again. Everyone would remember and he, Richard Pullman, would be famous along with it.

The first public electricity supply was introduced into Godalming in 1881 and so it became the first town to have electric street lights.

Godalming's Unfamous Residents

LORD THEODORE THADDEUS OCTAVIUS "RAHUL, OH-RAHUL" ADDAMS-SMYTHE-BENTWATERS

The nearly famous inventor who lived in Godalming from 1841

By Martyn Adams

Born: April 13th, 1839 (twice) in Peshawar, Pakistan.

Died: September 15th, 1899 after many attempts

Breeding

Lord Theodore Smythe-Bentwaters was born at a very young age to Lady Hortense Ophelia Addams-Smythe (1816 - ?) wife of Lord Octavius Ulysses Lucian Rickidicki Bentwaters (1801 - 1841). Theodore's father, Lord Octavious, was almost famous for his four foot wide moustache until it caught fire while smoking a cigar during a tiger hunt. Lord Theodore suffered minor burns, the tiger was unharmed but the mahout had to be treated for aching ribs.

Early Life

Lord Theodore was born in Pakistan, their only child. The family, including Lady Hortense's favourite gardener Rahul, moved to England in 1841 taking up residence in a house in Busbridge after Lord Octavius Bentwaters lost his fortune unsuccessfully suing his wife for divorce. She later sued him for losing all their money and won. Lord

Octavius, now penniless and forced to sleep in the conservatory, committed suicide by the very unusual method of self-garrotting after, apparently, shooting at himself several times and missing. He was not known as a good shot and neither was his wife.

Young Lord Theodore subsequently endured a deprived childhood growing up pretty much alone, apart from his nanny, two private tutors, the cook, butler, footmen, housemaids and several other servants who lived in the attic. The young Lord often reminisced that he couldn't sleep at night because of the pounding coming from upstairs. Thus he would spend many happy hours alone reading or playing with himself.

After his father's suicide his mother spent most of her time in London taking only her trusted gardener, Rahul, with her. She later married her divorce lawyer who, sadly, committed suicide some weeks later (in the same manner as his father). And thus the family fortunes were restored.

Later Life

In 1860 he obtained a regular allowance from his Mother, and thereafter allowed his staff and their families (most of whom were now married to each other) to move into the building proper while he occupied the basement. There he would spend his time creating inventions, writing doggerel and failing to learn to play the bassoon.

By 1880 Lord Theodore had very little money as he had been sued so many times because of his inventions.

Lord Theodore died in 1899. He narrowly survived drowning in January when pushed into the river Wey by a passer-by (believed to have once been a customer). He was stabbed in March but recovered (probably by another ex-customer). In May he was poisoned but he recovered from that too. He was twice shot in July, but both times the bullets missed vital organs and again, he survived. Sensing that his time was nearing its end Lord Theodore, as is traditional in the nobility, turned to religion. He also adopted the practice of wearing the family suit of armour and never left his house.

On September 15th, 1899 Lord Theodore was struck in the faceplate by a very fast, low flying heron through an open window. Police suspected fowl play.

Appendix A

During his lifetime at Godalming Lord Theodore was nearly famous for his many inventions.

Some of his less uncommercial inventions include: -

1862: The Gentleman's Unobtrusive Blouse Retaining Apparatus

Elastic braces worn under the crotch and attached to the bottom of shirts to keep them taught. Tended to chafe and snapped at the most inopportune time, often causing the wearer to shriek falsetto in agony.

1863: The Gentleman's Trouser Lifting Comfort Booster

An ingenious system of levers activated when the wearer sits. It gently pulls the trousers up from the knee preventing 'knee-stretched trouser syndrome.' When activated accidentally it caused much confusion and general hilarity.

1865: The Gentleman's Automatic Painless Toe Nail Trimming Foot Stocking Insert

Shaped sandpaper inserted into the end of socks to gently wear away one's toenails. Tendency to abrade the wearer's socks and also his toes, causing the wearer to wince while walking.

1867: The Gentleman's System for Discreet Vent-Silencing, Mal-odour Reduction and Leg Warming.

A leather tube with built in sound-baffle plates, inserted into the anus. The exhaust tube was then split into two, each downpipe strapped to the back of a leg. Painful to sit upon, but very popular with the older nobility who were often required to stand for long periods before Her Majesty, Queen Victoria.

It is believed that a custom device still exists in the Royal Attic at Windsor, but with the baffle plates removed and an oboe reed substituted, tuned to high E flat.

1869: The Gentleman's Head Warmer, Posture Encourager and Automated Hat Doffer

A steam driven device built into a top hat that automatically lifts when the wearer bows his head slightly. The boiler had a tendency to explode if it was not used at least once every fifteen minutes.

1870: The Gentleman's Quality Height Enhancing and Emergency Ruffian Avoidance Footwear.

A very short, shoe shaped, powerful spring embedded into the soles of custom designed shoes. Upon encountering ruffians (muggers) a lever is pulled and the wearer could leap over their heads and then run away.

Sadly the wearer was usually propelled sideways, striking a wall and rendering them unconscious - much to the delight of the ruffians.

It is rumoured that a Prussian Military Attaché accidentally triggered his footwear when clicking his heels before Her Majesty Queen Victoria. The hapless diplomat was nailed to the ceiling of Buckingham Palace by the point of his Pickelhaube. Her Majesty, and especially the French ambassador, were most amused. Prussia invaded France shortly thereafter.

MURDER MOST FOUL

By Ian Honeysett

What's that – am I Isaac Woods? Yes, sir, that's me - Constable of the Parish of Godalming. You've been keen to meet me, you say? Yes, sir, that chair's free – please join me. Especially if you're buying the drinks. So let me guess what you want to talk about. Those terrible murders back in1817 when it's fair to say I played a crucial part in one of the most appalling events in the history of this fine town. The foul murder of old Mr George Chennell and his housekeeper, Bet Wilson. A few years ago now but still fresh in my mind as though it were yesterday.

What's that – what am I drinking? Well that's very kind of you, sir. Make mine a pint of porter if you please and I'll tell you the tale if you've a few minutes. It's quite fitting, in fact, that we're sat here in The Richmond Arms as this here public house played quite a crucial role in the whole sorry business…

Ah, that's a lovely pint, that is… Now, where was I? Ah, yes. It was the morning of, let me see, I think it was… ah yes, thanks for reminding me – my memory's not what it was… 11th November 1817. Well, it was about seven in the morning when this fellow, I think his name was Tom Witley, called at the house on the High Street of old George Chennell, the shoemaker, to see if his shoes were ready. He was an excellent shoemaker was George. In fact I always got my shoes there. Bit expensive, especially on a constable's wage but you've got to pay for quality I always say. And, no, I didn't get an allowance for footwear although I walked a fair few miles in the course of my job I did.

Anyway, I digress. So Tom goes to knock on the door when he sees it's already open. He calls out for Mr Chennell but there's no reply. Then he notices an odd smell. Sort of metallic smell. So he pushes open the door rather nervously and looks in. And what a sight greets his eyes! There, stretched out on the floor is poor old Bet Wilson, the housekeeper! The floor's covered in blood. Blood everywhere. No wonder as her throat's been cut in a most shocking manner. He shouts out for old Mr Chennell again and now is fearing the worst. Naturally he's not keen to go inside on his own so he goes and calls some of the neighbours and, with them, they make their way very cautiously into the house and then upstairs. The smell is overpowering as they open the door to the main bedroom. And there, lying by his bed, is poor old George with his head very nearly severed from his body. And, of course, there's blood everywhere. His body is covered in bruises and it's clear the poor old soul put up quite a fight. Now one of the neighbours knows a bit about death, having served in the wars against Bonaparte, and touches the body and says it's quite cold. So they reckon these terrible murders must have been committed the previous night.

Anyway, they have a look around in case there are any more bodies and, thank goodness, they're aren't. So they go back downstairs and take a closer look at Bet Wilson and there, lying beside her body, is a hammer, Mr Chennell's hammer, all covered in blood. And it's clear now that poor Bet's skull has been smashed to pieces. Almost beyond recognition.

What's that – another pint? Well that's exceedingly good of you. I don't normally have more than…but, since you offered…another pint of porter would do nicely.

Ah, that's a lovely pint. Now, did I mention all the blood? I did. Well, they quickly made their way to my house of course to report what they had discovered. Fortunately I'd finished my breakfast and I soon joined them as we made our way back to the scene of this abominable crime. I was able to confirm all they had told me and so I reported the murders to the Magistrates who instructed me to investigate immediately. What's that, was it all down to me? Well, I'm not saying it was just me but I certainly did the lion's share as anyone who knows will tell you. I quickly identified anyone who witnessed anything at all. It took some doing I can tell you. But I've never been afraid of hard work. In all I must have spoken to over thirty people and it was soon clear that poor old Mr Chennell's son, George, was the main suspect. Yes, both called George. Confusing at times.

So I brought him in for questioning by the Magistrates. He denied any knowledge of what had happened of course. He said he had been drinking in this very public house and left briefly around nine o'clock that Monday night. It was reckoned that the foul murders took place between nine and ten. Said he had left his pipe on the table and it was still alight when he returned so he couldn't have been gone long. A real drinker he was. Dissolute, that's the word. And it was common knowledge he didn't get on at all well with his father or his house-keeper. Many's the time he could be heard using the most obscene language about her in particular. He seemed to have a real grudge against Bet Wilson. No idea why. She was a sweet old soul. But, at that stage, the evidence was still limited and the Coroner's inquest the next day found it was a case of Wilful Murder by Persons Unknown.

Then we identified an accomplice: old Mr Chennell's carman, one William Chalcraft. He was a bad one, he was. Even worse character than the son, who was an old associate of his. Well, working with the Magistrates, we put together a veritable trail of evidence that was as water-tight as you can get. I was applauded for all my hard work I was. Mind you, it took several months before it finally went to trial on 12th August 1818. I'll never forget that date. Just about the whole of Godalming was there. The leading counsel for the Crown, Mr Gurney, gave a marvellous speech. Couldn't have done much better myself. He stressed just how dreadful a crime it was. Not just wilful murder but by the son against his aged father and the servant against his master.

Why did they do it? Well, old Mr Chennell was a respectable tradesman of course. But he wasn't just a shoemaker, he had considerable wealth. He owned a lot of property including a farm. And he was good to his son too. Although they didn't live together, young George often took his meals at his father's house. There was plenty of evidence against the two of them. The morning the bodies were found, Chalcraft went into the house very early but claimed he saw nothing whereas there was no way he could have missed the body of poor old Bet. And he was heard to say his master had been murdered before anyone had been upstairs and found his body. And, when they searched Chennell's lodgings, they found two pound notes which a witness swore he had paid old Mr Chennell and they were spattered with blood! And, what's more, the son had been quite unable to pay a bill of 8 ½ pence that very Monday morning. Yet, after the murders, he was back in the Richmond Arms drinking till late. And when the two of them were asked where they were that Monday evening, they both claimed they had not seen each other since the previous Friday. An obvious lie as several witnesses had seen them together.

Was there a woman involved, you ask? Oh yes. One Sarah Hurst. A known accomplice of the two of them. Now the son had said he left the public house that evening to meet with Sarah – he was separated from his wife and everyone knew he and Chalcraft were very friendly with Sarah, if you know what I mean. And several witnesses said they saw Sarah stood by the alleyway to old Mr Chennell's house around nine fifteen that night. She was their lookout. But she did for them both, did Sarah. Not at first of course as she accused two utterly blameless individuals of the crime but I soon proved that was a downright lie.

Sarah was so overcome at the trial she could hardly stand up. She said that Chalcraft had asked her if she would meet him that Monday evening which she agreed to do. He asked her to stand by old Mr Chennell's house to watch, which she did for some time. She wasn't sure how long she was there. After Chalcraft came out the house, she heard a screech from within. She asked what the two of them had been up to and Chalcraft said: "We have done for them both." She saw blood on his frock sleeves. She asked how it came there and Chalcraft replied: "It was the blood from them two." The following night, she was in the Angel Inn with Chalcraft and he offered her £4 to keep it all a secret. She refused saying she would not have it.

Though I say as shouldn't, I played something of a star role in the trial as it was I who showed the court the fatal knife with a wooden handle still covered in blood. There was a shudder around the court when I did so. And then I produced old Mr Chennell's hammer, his shoemaker's hammer, all covered in blood too. It was sharp at one end and round and blunt at the other and the wounds on poor old Bet Wilson's head matched the shape of that hammer exactly. Exactly.

Well there was no doubt about their guilt after that. They had no defence at all. They blathered on about things of no consequence like that pipe still burning when the son returned to the Richmond Arms. Oh Chalcraft protested that he was as innocent as a child unborn of course. But do you know how long it took the jury to find them both guilty? Three minutes! That's all. Then the judge sentenced them both to be taken to the prison from whence they came and, on the following Friday, to be carried to the place of execution back in Godalming – on the Lammas lands, just behind the Parish church – and there to be hung by the neck till dead. Their bodies were then to be taken and dissected according to statute. And may the Lord have mercy on their souls. The nice thing is that they used the wood from the gallows when they repaired the church steeple. Waste not, want not I always say.

Yes, it was a moment I – and most of the good people of Godalming who were there – will never forget. Nor will we forget the hangings themselves of course. The very last time we ever had public hangings in the town, sadly. That was on 14th August. Interesting thing is they both seemed quite calm and composed. Almost as if they expected someone to intervene at the last moment and stop the executions. No, neither of them ever confessed. The son was drinking his beer and smoking his pipe with as much relish both in Horsemonger Lane gaol and at Kingston as though he had nothing to trouble his conscience. Chalcot admitted nothing as if he was waiting for his accomplice to confess first. People said they had made a compact to admit nothing in the hope of acquittal.

Chalcraft left a wife and six children, three from a former marriage. They said his first wife died a victim to his licentious habits and that his second wife he met in the workhouse where he was sent to be cured. Chennell, the son, left one child who lived with his grandfather. As they waited to be taken to Godalming to the scaffold, they were apparently offered one more chance to confess and repent but both declared their innocence. The Reverend read the 51st and 90th psalms and then then from the Book of Job, I think, and that passage on the Last Judgement where the sheep are separated from the goats. Quite moving I'm sure. Chennell, they say, seemed more concerned about a fly buzzing round his head than the fate of his immortal soul. Kept on yawning. Then the wagon arrived to take them to their execution. I was waiting there, of course. I saw them brought out with irons on their legs and their hands pinioned and the rope that was to seal their miserable fate around their waists.

What were they wearing? Well, Chennell was dressed as at his trial in a black jockey coat, a striped waistcoat and grey, cotton pantaloons. Chalcraft had on a new frock coat. Quite smart they were. Well it was their big day I suppose.

The crowds lining the streets were immense. I've never seen so many smocks and straw hats!

The procession arrived at the Lammas lands around eleven in the morning. The gallows had been erected inside a ring made of rope. The Reverend Mann asked if they wished to communicate anything but, again, they both declined and continued to protest their innocence although it was said that Chalcraft had said he would "tell the whole pedigree of it" before his death. Chennell ascended the platform first and asked for the cap to be drawn over his eyes to prevent his face from being seen by all those who knew him. He stood calm but Chalcraft was all atremble.

Then the platform was pulled from under them and so both were launched into eternity. Both struggled a little but the hangman was quick to pull down their heels with some force and soon it was all over. Their bodies were left to hang for an hour and then given to Mr Parsons and Mr Haynes, two local surgeons, for dissection. Their bodies were then taken by waggon to the house where they had perpetrated their terrible crimes and one of them was placed on the very spot where poor old Bet Wilson had been found murdered. A nice touch that, I thought. In fact it was I who suggested it. Then the two surgeons performed the first stage of dissection and the bodies were left in this state so that anyone interested might see. A salutary warning to anyone tempted to repeat such horrible acts.

Yes, a day to remember most assuredly. Ah, I seem to have finished that excellent pint. Thirsty work all this talking.

Was that the end of it, you ask? Well, not quite. Though I'm not certain I can continue without a little more… Oh, that's very kind of you, sir. Yes, I think I might just manage a final pint of porter. Most unusual for me to drink three pints but I can see you're eager to hear it all.

Well, it seems that these may not have been the only murders carried out by Chennell and Chalcraft. They were both present at the scene of two previous killings. One was in Petersfield and another in Farnham where the murder knife found appeared to be one of old Mr Chennell's. They probably thought they led charmed lives and would never pay the penalty. And perhaps they would have got away with these foul murders if I hadn't happened to be the constable here in Godalming. Who is to say?

What's that? Have I any doubts at all that they were guilty? None whatsoever, sir. You've heard the evidence and I've only told you the half of it. Yes, I know they protested their innocence to the very end and seemed to believe that someone or something would intervene to save their wretched necks. But they were surely as guilty as we are sat here.

What's that you say – have I heard the story of the woman from the prison coach? Oh, yes, I heard that a few years after all this. An absurd tale. It was said that there was a woman convict on one of the prison coaches that used to stop at The Kings Arms in Godalming on the way to Portsmouth for transportation to Australia. The story went that she had a deep hatred for the Chennell family because of some terrible wrong they had done to her family. That she arranged with one of the guards to be let out on the very evening of the murders and somehow persuaded or bribed Chennell and Chalcraft to lead her to the house and keep watch while she robbed old Mr Chennell. But that her plan all along was to murder him and his house-keeper and to put the blame on Chalcraft and the son. In this way she could extract revenge on both Chennells. She then returned to her confinement in The Kings Arms and, the following day, carried on to Portsmouth from whence she was transported to Australia – having stolen a considerable amount of money from the older Mr Chennell.

All nonsense of course! Not a shred of evidence and as full of holes as you could imagine. No, I have no doubt whatsoever that they were the murderers and met their just fate. Many a guilty man has protested his innocence to the end. No, it was my greatest case and I am proud, sir, of the role I played. A role in which I was heartily commended by both the Magistrates and the Judge, I might add.

What's that you say? Speak up, sir, all this porter must be affecting my hearing.

I said, Constable Woods, that the woman from the prison coach is called Grace Hanozet and that she is now living in New South Wales in some comfort thanks to recovering at least part of the Chennell fortune which was so cruelly stolen from her family.

And how do you know this, sir?

I know this, sir, because I am her brother, formerly a guard on the prison coaches.

Why, sir, if I should believe you for one moment, I would arrest you as an accomplice in those foul murders! But, as it is, you have generously bought me three pints of porter and I doubt I am capable of such an arrest just now. And given my good name, such as it is, rests largely on my success in bringing those two to justice, I decline to believe you, sir. But I wouldn't say no to another pint!

The last public hanging was held in Godalming – at the green area adjacent to the Lammas Land and Borough Road.

I'M SORRY BUT…

By Heather Wright

"Bernice I am shattered. I just have to sit down."

She looked at me with some concern.

"Then it's time to have a coffee and a snacky lunch," she said.

We were in America on the second floor of Nordstom's, a large Harrod's like store in Downtown Seattle and had been wandering round for just a moment too long. The store wasn't full but the restaurant was packed. We were on holiday from Godalming.

"You have to get your food first," Bee said as she grabbed a tray. We had decided that we just needed a sandwich and a coffee as we were booked for a fairly early dinner that evening.

"Well I'm going to get a table," I said, "so find me".

I went to the seating area and spoke to the attendant who was showing people to their tables.

"My daughter is in the queue," I said "but I am feeling rather rough and desperately need to sit down, could you find me a table please?"

She looked at me, obviously taking in the white hair and the pained expression…

"Of course."

She saw a table just being vacated and pointed to it saying that she was sure I wouldn't mind that it wasn't yet cleared.

"Thank you."

I sat down feeling my whole body echoing the thanks as I leaned forward and put my head in my hands for a moment.

"Excuse me Madam," said a harsh, American, male voice, "the policy of this restaurant is that you can't sit at a table until you have your food".

I looked up to see a young waiter in a white jacket glowering at me.

He had obviously had a charm by-pass.

"Yes I do realise that," I replied, "but wasn't feeling well so the very kind lady over there showed me to this table. My daughter is in the queue and should be here with our lunch any minute now."

"Well it's not allowed," he repeated.

"I do understand," I replied, "but I'm afraid I am staying put."

At which he huffed off once more with a click of his tongue.

I put my head back in my hands, quite consciously this time but he was back quicksticks.

"There is no-one on their own in the queue," he whinged, "so I will have to ask you to move because the policy of this restaurant is that you can't sit down without food."

He was beginning to really irritate me now.

"Well you have a choice," I said, "you can leave me here waiting for my daughter and lunch or you can go and get me an ambulance."

He huffed off again and went to report me to the General Manager who arrived at my table with a big gold badge indicating who she was.

But not only had she obviously been to charm school, she was stunning. Tall and blonde with a lovely figure and warm eyes she crouched down beside my seat and said…

I knew the script by now.

"I'm afraid that the policy of this restaurant is that you…"

"I know," I replied. "But as I have explained, I was feeling really rough and desperately needed to sit down".

"Where are you from?" she asked with obvious interest having heard me speak.

"The UK."

Her lovely eyes lit up.

"My Dad lives in the UK," she said.

"Is he English then?"

"No but he went over there some years ago and fell in love and has lived there ever since."

She was really excited and I felt energised by her enthusiasm.

"Where does your Dad live?" I asked.

"Oh. In Surrey".

"I live in Surrey. Which part of Surrey does he live?"

"Near Guildford," she replied.

"I live near Guildford so where exactly does he live?"

"Godalming – and she named the street."

I grinned.

"Well, this is amazing because that is just across the road from my house. What a coincidence."

She was so delighted.

"I'm getting married in two weeks," she told me, "and my Dad can't come to the wedding because his wife's mother is ill. Would you mind giving him a ring when you get home to tell him you have seen me and I am looking well?"

"I'll be glad to," I replied.

By now Bernice had arrived expecting to see me looking distraught and instead seeing me buzzing. She told me later that she was greeted by Mr Grumpy and had told him she needed to find her Mum (Mom) who was feeling tired and not at all well. He pointed to where I was sitting whereupon she became quite embarrassed as, she said I looked as if I had already had two coffees and was ready to do a workout.

She just commented that I was obviously feeling a lot better but he was unimpressed!

Tammy introduced herself, we brought Bee up to date and Tammy gave me the name and number of her father in Godalming.

"I am *so* pleased we met," she said, "I'm sure it was meant to be. And thank you."

Bernice and I mulled over the story while we had our coffee and sandwiches and then, about ten minutes later, Mr Grumpy himself appeared with two beautiful dishes of Crème Brulee.

"With the compliments of the General Manager" he said putting them down.

And then my cup runneth over!

Of course I rang her father when I got home, spoke to his wife first and then told him that I had seen Tammy.

He was so pleased and it made me think I must stop moaning that my sons live a long way away as Birmingham or York. They are next door compared with the distance between Godalming and Seattle.

ELECTRICITY

By Christine Butler

(Technical information about early electricity supply in Godalming from 'The Brilliant Ray' by Francis Haveron, Craddocks 1981)

In September 1881 the first public supply of electricity in the world was switched on in Godalming, illuminating the centre of the town with three arc lights. The electricity was provided by a water-powered generator on a mill-leate from the River Wey. With a monopoly in the town, the Godalming Gas and Coke Company Ltd kept increasing their charges for supplying gas and Godalming Borough Council thought the new-fangled electricity would prove to be cheaper than gas for the town's street lighting.

The Council arranged with a London firm for an experimental electricity supply to be set up, with the help of the owner of a local tannery business, R & J Pullman Ltd, operating at Westbrook Mills. There was already a weir with a water wheel situated in a small building near the main tannery and this was where the generator was installed. This experiment with hydro-electricity was not a success as the flow of the river proved too erratic. Steam power was used as an alternative for driving the dynamos, with some success, but there were other problems. Not enough townspeople wanted electric lighting in their homes and businesses to make the scheme pay. In 1884 the decision was made by the Council to revert to gas following an acceptable tender from the Gas Company. They reduced the cost, installed better lights and the quality of the gas improved too. Not until 1897 did electricity illuminate the streets of Godalming again.

In September 1981, a year after we moved to the Godalming area, a rally of boats was held on the River Wey in Godalming, as part of the Godalming Electricity Centenary celebrations. Our small cruiser 'Someday' was moored at Farncombe Boathouse then. The rally site was half a mile up-river from there, above Catteshall Lock.

The boat rally was organised in conjunction with the Inland Waterways Association. As we were members we volunteered to help and were asked to act as marshals on the Sunday, in the flood-meadow to be used as a car park. That proved quite entertaining on Sunday afternoon, when people started making for home and tried to drive their cars out of the mud. Many drivers did not seem to have a clue about manoeuvring in slippery conditions. Four-wheeled drive vehicles were not common then, of course, but luckily someone appeared with a tractor. He was in great demand for towing cars out.

Saturday had started bright and sunny for the events on that day. The official opening of the Centenary celebrations was scheduled for seven thirty at the Pepperpot in Godalming. I am not sure now whether it went ahead as planned or not. That evening, during a performance by the Mikron Theatre Company at the rally site, thunder started rumbling around. The storm broke with terrific ferocity. Torrential rain fell and the wind howled in the trees. The audience leaving the theatre marquee were soaked.

We decided not to venture up through Catteshall Lock in our boat on Sunday morning to moor at the rally site and walked there from the boathouse instead. That turned out to be a wise decision in spite of the continuing showers. So much rain had fallen the previous night that the water level in the river had risen alarmingly by Sunday afternoon. Sensible boat-owners made an early start for home, before navigation became dangerous in the fast-flowing floodwater. A few were extremely foolhardy, waiting till later to move off downstream.

After the rally closed, the river was declared unsafe for navigation. We had retreated to our little boat, thankfully still safe on its mooring, for a warming cup of tea out of the rain. As we sat in our cabin we could see sizeable narrow boats being swept past with their helmsmen struggling to control them. How many managed to descend deep Unstead Lock that evening I do not know but miraculously the lock escaped serious damage.

That was not the case with two of the narrow boats, Nancy Bell and L'Hedoniste, on their home moorings at Farncombe Boathouse. They were tied up next to each other on the opposite side of the peninsula of land to our boat. Neither craft had been taken to the rally site, though Nancy Larcombe had a stall at the rally selling some of her landscape paintings. When she and her family returned to Nancy Bell, after the Saturday evening Mikron performance, they found that the old alder tree to which the boat was tied had been blown down in the storm.

Nancy gives an account of what happened in her book, 'It's a Boat's Life'. Two American tourists with a canoe, who were camping nearby on the peninsula, said that the boat had been pulled over by the tree as it crashed into the river, but had righted itself and was not damaged. Unfortunately the interior was a mess where everything had been thrown about and it was some time before they had sorted out the chaos and tidied up enough to go to bed.

The owners of the other boat were less fortunate. When we walked along the peninsula past the boathouse we saw a scene of devastation, with bits of branches and other debris lying around and people securing the battered covers on their boats. Across the stern of L'Hedoniste, holding it down, was the fallen alder tree. It had let water into the engine compartment and bent the stern railing. That took a great deal of sorting out. The rally was certainly a memorable event for many people.

In May 2008 Godalming became the first market town in Britain to provide public wireless access in the town centre – 125 years after it was first to have a public electric supply...

Godalming's Unfamous Residents

JEREMIAH BASCOM DINKWORTH

Godalming's least successful business tycoon.

By Martyn Adams

Born: October 3rd, 1902 in Godalming, Surrey.

Died: February 14th, 1958

EARLY LIFE

Jeremiah Dinkworth was born a Hindu to a Protestant family in their Godalming home while his mother wasn't looking. However, two weeks later, his father (Sergeant Major David Arthur Dinkworth) was delighted with his new son. He was informed while in transit returning home after serving two years in the Boer War (1899 - 1902). Within his first year Jeremiah and his parents were all persuaded to convert to the Church of England because of the sheer beauty of the nearby Church of St Peter and St Paul (which has always remained stationary and can still be found in Godalming to this very day). Furthermore the rector of the church (renown locally for his love of firearms) was said to have been very persuasive at around that time.

Jeremiah attended the local schools but was not a particularly memorable child. In fact few people remembered him attending any of them. Furthermore his teachers had difficulty remembering him even when shown the old school registers or when he was pointed out in photographs.

Jeremiah's early years were spent in his father's tailoring business, unsuccessfully learning the trade. He married Cynthia Eagerbend after a lightning romance at the age of twenty one within just two months of their first meeting. They had their first child (Earnest) five months later.

Jeremiah later tried taking up carpentry but that resulted in many accidents, most of which involved his left thumb.

LATER LIFE

Having extensively studied the successes of the American business magnates such as Henry Ford (1863 - 1947) and Erastus Corning (1794 - 1872), Jeremiah, after his twenty seventh birthday, decided that he too would attempt fame and fortune. After studying economic theory and the operations of the stock market he invested all his savings and his inheritance from his father's estate. The stock market crash of 1929, just one week later, put paid to his immediate plans, but sadly - did not shake his confidence.

In 1935/36 Jeremiah created an aircraft factory in a local farmer's barn. The plan was to manufacture the tandem winged, French designed HM14 'Flying Flea' under licence and sell the aircraft to the relatively prosperous inhabitants of Godalming. He reasoned that if he sold enough the council would then be obliged to build the airfield needed to support them. It's unclear as to how he intended to convince the authorities in London to build a suitable receiving aerodrome.

Jeremiah was classified as unfit to become a test pilot due to his enormous, flat, left thumb. With little capital, no knowledge of aerodynamics and little skill at carpentry Jeremiah's attempts at improving and simplifying the aeroplane's design proved to be fatal for his test pilot, the farmer. Furthermore the second, almost complete, prototype HM14 was raped to destruction by the farmer's prize bull.

From mid-1935 through to 1941 Jeremiah started many other business ventures, none of which had the success he'd hoped for. All were based from his small flat above his family's tailoring shop in Godalming High Street.

When World War two started and, upon learning that men up to the age of 41 could be conscripted (especially if unmarried), Mrs. Cynthia Dinkworth sued Jeremiah for divorce. Jeremiah fortunately managed to have his 42nd birthday before they could draft him. Cynthia gave up.

During the second world war Jeremiah served with the Home Guard but was not a particularly memorable soldier. In fact few people remembered him attending any of the training / drills / military exercises. Moreover his officers had difficulty remembering him, even when shown unit documentation or when pointed out in photographs.

Jeremiah died of natural causes in 1958. Few people remembered the funeral, even when shown the photographs.

Appendix A: Jeremiah's Least Forgettable Companies

1936: The Dinkworth Bicycle Manufacturing Company Ltd

Jeremiah built a bicycle from part of the framework of one of the destroyed 'Flying Flea's. He sold it to a neighbour. Encouraged by this he started constructing a second.

1936: The Dinkworth Motor Bicycle Manufacturing Company Ltd

After his neighbour returned the original bicycle as

being uncomfortable, unsuitable and unsafe, Jeremiah mounted the engine from the Flying Flea into the frame and resold it to the same person.

1937: The Dinkworth Sports Car Manufacturing Ltd

After inheriting several items of furniture and the bent motor cycle from his neighbour (after a fatal road accident) Jeremiah built a car chassis and re-used the engine. The new prototype four seater sports car was known as the Dinkworthy Dinkle Mk 1. The interior design of this vehicle was unusual as the rear seat was a well upholstered settee. The vehicle had a miniature chandelier which hung from the centre of the roof and a small log fire built into the rear of the front passenger seat, complete with a small wooden mantel shelf and side mounted chimney. Rear seat passengers did complain about continually having to duck to avoid the swinging chandelier and the front passengers often complained about the heat, but Jeremiah was reluctant to give up one of the vehicle's unique selling points.

1937: Dinkworth Car Sales

This company was tasked with the sale of the sports car prototype as no-one had shown interest in the car to date. The Dinkle Mk 1 was promoted as the only sports car in the world in which the passengers could enjoy freshly made toast during the journey.

1937: Dinkworth Budget Petroleum Supply Ltd

This company was formed in the hope that cheaper petrol might encourage local residents to purchase his sports car.

1937: The Dinkworth Coachworks and Motor Cycle Side Car Manufacturing Company Ltd

After a road traffic accident (caused by smoke from burnt toast obscuring the driver's vision), Jeremiah reconstructed the original motorbike and used the remaining half of the Dinkle Mk 1 to form the basis of a sidecar. The chandelier was omitted but the fireplace was retained. The combination was marketed as the only motorcycle / sidecar in the world in which the passenger could enjoy freshly made toast.

1938: Dinkworth's Fire Extinguishers Ltd

Jeremiah formed this company from his experiences after the sidecar caught fire during a demonstration.

1938: Dinkworth's Scrap Wood and Metal Merchants

Unable to make progress with his earlier companies, and under some pressure from his wife, Jeremiah sold all his assets, although it was rumoured that Mrs. Dinkworth's ample lingerie fetched the most money.

1939: Dinkworth's Used Tea Bag Brokering Ltd

Until 1940 it was unclear why Jeremiah invested so heavily in acquiring used tea bags. Nevertheless he managed to obtain a considerable quantity for a very reasonable price during this period. He managed to accrue nearly three tons of tea bags which he kept in his flat. It was then that, for reasons unclear, his wife finally left him.

1940: Dinkworth's Instant Sun Tan Bathing Emporium

Jeremiah opened the bathroom of his flat as a Sun Tan Bathing Emporium. The idea was that after just a few minutes of bathing in his luke-warm secret formula

'Magical Sun Tanning Fluids', the bather would acquire an instant healthy sun tan. The Sun Tan Bathing Emporium had to close when it was discovered that bathers were unable to submerge their knees or their heads at the same time into the secret formula and thus when they came out they weren't tanned in these locations. Furthermore, one or two customers stayed too long and found themselves dyed a very unfashionable, very dark but noticeably uneven colour.

1940: Dinkworth's Natural Leather Tanning Works

Jeremiah tried unsuccessfully using the tanning process on anything else inanimate but there was little demand.

1941: Dinkworth's Business Consulting Ltd

Jeremiah tried marketing his extensive business knowledge he had acquired over the previous few years. It soon became clear that the war time economy really had no need for his experience. Had he tried stand-up comedy he might have been significantly more successful – but that's not saying much.

Godalming had its first purpose-built fire station in 1816 in Moss Lane. It was a small brick built shed with a low bell tower to house a single engine.

A TRIP TO ENTEBBE AIRPORT UGANDA

By Capt. Ron Macdonald FRAeS AC rtd.

The night was dark and stormy and we were 33,000ft. over the Alps en route to Paris when the no 1 engine low pressure warning light came on with an increase in oil temperature so we shut it down. How different it all seems from Thursley, Godalming where we've now lived for these past 24 years.

But let's go back a bit, I was a DC 8 Captain on reserve when Scheduling called and asked how I would like a 5 day trip?

"Sounds good to me" I said. "Where am I going?"

"Well", said the scheduler, "it's to London then Dead Head Paris then to Nairobi then from there to Uganda to evacuate some Asians on behalf of the UN".

So, on September the 24th 1972 I operated flight YUL to Heathrow with a Douglas DC 8 jet airliner No 807 and then, with my crew, we carried on to Paris Orly airport as passengers with Air France. We departed Orly on the 26th direct to Nairobi via Italy then on to Bengazi as we were not permitted over the United Arab Republic or Chad and, after an 8 hour trip, we landed at Nairobi airport which happened to have Canadian Air Traffic Controllers on duty.

We proceeded to our hotel: the flight crew and four male pursers - the company was concerned that female cabin staff might be in danger in Uganda.

Checking in at the hotel, I noticed a Caledonian crew at the desk with a figure in the Captain's uniform looking a bit familiar so I went over to say hello and found we had been Sea Cadets on HMS Vulture St. Merryn, Cornwall on a two week summer camp during 1946.

He asked what I was doing and, on advising him of our operation to rescue the Asians from Uganda, he said that, when we contact Entebbe, if they say confirm your pressurisation is normal, don't land.

Shortly afterwards I received a phone call from the Canadian Ambassador in Uganda asking if I could give a definite landing time at Entebbe so that he could escort the school buses carrying our passengers to the airport. He also advised that he would be in a white Mercedes with a Canadian flag on the roof. So 13.30hrs was decided on.

When we got to the airport to prepare for our flight to Uganda, the promised 2 cases of oil for the Rolls Royce Conways, supposedly put on board in Orly was missing, and, in discussion with the PAA agent- come mechanic, he pointed out that East African Airlines operated the VC 10 which was also RR Conway powered. So he took me over to their base where I requested 2 cases of RR Conway oil. They looked at my Canadian dollars with suspicion (the company had given me $5000 for incidentals), so I offered to complete a form for the oil, signing it *"Pierre Elliot Trudeau per Capt. Ron Macdonald"*.

The flight over Lake Victoria to Entebbe was uneventful and, as we approached the airport, the First Officer said he could see the school buses and the white Mercedes nearing the airport. There was some apprehension as we approached the terminal as we could see a lot of military personnel and, when we parked the plane, I left the no. 3 engine running until I was assured of an air start as we had no Air-Start Power Unit on board. I opened the forward door to be met by a 6ft Ugandan soldier pointing his rifle at me but, pushing past, was a PAA agent who said he had an air-start, so we could shut down the engines.

The School buses had arrived and boarding the passengers began immediately. Then the PAA agent gave me a telex from Heathrow dispatch stating they were unable to arrange a landing in Italy for fuel but had got permission for a fuel stop in Athens. The navigator and I looked at the charts and worked out the distance from Entebbe to Athens : it was about a 7 hour flight as again we had to fly to Bengazi before heading east for Athens.

There was some minor harassing of the passengers by the Ugandan troops but the Canadian High Commissioner used his influence to keep the flow of passengers moving. With the Athens fuel stop, we were now to be at maximum take-off weight at a temperature of 28 degrees so we opted to take-off to the south over the lake for a more stable surface temperature then turned north heading towards massive thunderstorms (as an aside we crossed the equator 4 times in 24 hours) so with the radar on, we wandered around and then asked the navigator for a heading to Bengazi and he said to turn left 4 degrees.

The approach to Athens was quite interesting - curving in over the harbour and lining up on the Instrument Landing System where the runway seemed surrounded by confusing lights. So I stayed heads down to 200ft. to ensure a safe landing on the runway.

After reaching the ramp and shutting down, we were met by elements of the Greek Army with an officer demanding to know who had given us permission to land at Athens? So I produced the telex from LHR dispatch and he calmed down but still kept his armed men at the bottom of the boarding stairs.

A representative of Olympic Airlines then arrived and he arranged for a fuel uplift and gave me a message from

LHR now advising us that we could not land at Orly because of no landings allowed after 23.30. So we now had to plan to land at Le Bourget. We fuelled up, got some fresh water and off we went to Le Bourget Paris. Then, while cruising at 33,000 ft. over the Alps, the number 1 engine oil pressure light came on with a rise in oil temperature, so we shut it down.

The approach to Le Bourget was again interesting as it seemed totally surrounded by the lights of the city of Paris and, on shutting down and deplaning, I was met by the Captain for the next leg to Montreal who asked "Where the hell have you been Ron?" I explained and told him "You won't be going anywhere for a while as I had to shut down number 1 engine due low oil pressure." With that me and my crew left for a well-earned rest.

On returning to Montreal I gave back the £5000 to Captain Bill Irving, my boss, telling him that I had signed a form for the oil with *"Pierre Elliot Trudeau"*. He almost had a fit but then we had a good laugh but I was told never use the Prime Minister's name again.

It had been an interesting trip and some of the stories our passengers told the Flight Attendants were pretty harrowing. They thanked us all for flying into Uganda to evacuate them from the on-going terror of Idi Amin.

Just as a small note, I had told my wife, Marge, that I was off to London then Paris for 4 days so, when I got back home, she asked me how was Paris? So I replied " Just the usual". She answered "Then how come your name was mentioned on the CBC news as having successfully rescued 142 Asians from Uganda?"

So what could I say? Except that I didn't want to worry her.

THE TSAR OF ALL THE ROOSHIAS

By Ian Honeysett

James Moon took one final swig of his second tot of brandy and pronounced "breakfast was done." Undoubtedly the highlight of his long tenure as landlord of The King's Arms (otherwise known as "the Moons") in Godalming High Street was about to take place. It had now been officially confirmed: tomorrow they would be hosting their most famous guest since Henry the Eighth (though James had not been present for that one). None other than Peter, Tsar of all the Russias and a small entourage (only around 20 in all) known as the "Grand Embassy". The full Embassy was 250 strong so this entourage comprised only his closest advisers. They were on an 18 month fact-finding tour of Western Europe to identify all the latest developments and bring Russia into the modern age. Top of their list was shipbuilding and the Russians were in Portsmouth where King William lll had given them free rein to visit the Royal Navy dockyard. He had even given Peter a ship – the Royal Transport- so keen was he to foster trade with Russia.

It was March 1698 which was, of course, the very month when Jeremy Collier's pamphlet, A Short View of the Immorality and Profaneness of the English Stage, was published. But James Moon was far too busy for that. There was a great deal to do to make ready for the visit. He had been briefed by some jumped-up Court official who explained that Peter was not simply Tsar of Russia but of Astrakhan and Siberia and Grand Prince of Smolensk, Sovereign of the Circassian and Mountain

Princes among many, many other titles. However, on this occasion, Peter was travelling incognito, as Peter Mikhail. Incognito was not easy given the size of his entourage and the fact that he was 6 feet 8 inches tall when the average height of European men was 5 feet 6 inches. James made a note to make sure he had a chair and a bed big enough. His favourite tipple was said to be a cup of brandy laced with pepper. Not, it had to be said, one of the most popular drinks in Godalming at that time.

James and his son, Joseph, had been severely warned not to stare at the Tsar as his appearance might seem rather odd to some. For such a tall man, he had a surprisingly small head and shoulders, hands and feet. He also had an odd facial tic and was said to suffer from petit mal, a form of epilepsy. The final advice was that the Russians had vast appetites for food and drink. Think of what a vast appetite might mean and then double it. James put Joseph in charge of the catering so that he could concentrate on ensuring everything else was "shipshape" as it were. James chortled at his little joke. Given Peter's interest in ships, it seemed an apt description. Joseph seemed unimpressed. Perhaps, he thought, he should lay in a few more quarts of brandy and mulled wine and sack. And a case of claret of course. Nothing but the best for the Russians, after all, they could afford it. With the profit from this visit, he might even be able to afford a short holiday. He felt he was due one as his last had been ten years ago.

By 2 o'clock the following day, a large crowd had gathered outside the King's Arms. The local pickpocket, Charlie Evans, was having a field day. A Royal visit, after all, was almost as popular as a public hanging. You had to find your entertainment where you could. Sidney and Amelia Clackett were treating the assembled to some favourite songs by Henry Purcell. They even had one ditty they claimed was in Russian but since nobody had any idea what Russian sounded like, this was unverifiable.

Suddenly a small urchin came running down the High Street shouting "He's here, he's here, the Sir of all the Rooshias is here!" People rapidly appeared from all the local shops and houses to get a glimpse of the Russian giant. Fellow publicans from The Red Lion, The Great George and the Angel were all there, ready to step in if the Moons ran out of supplies.

The coaches pulled up and the Clacketts began singing their latest ballad which so happened to be about the royal visitor. The chorus was, claimed Sidney, in Russian. Unfortunately, it had been raining heavily lately and the first coach managed to drench them and a dozen others as it careered through a very large and muddy puddle.

James and Joseph Moon stepped up to the coach door which was flung open by Tsar Peter's Major Domo, Count Kornilov. He was impressive both in bulk and dress. Not to mention an elaborate moustache which would have resembled a walrus had James and Joseph ever seen a walrus. He embraced both of them together and would no doubt have kissed them on most of their cheeks had they not managed to escape.

"I am Count Kornilov," he declared proudly. "You will deal with me in all matters to do with our visit. You understand? "

"Of course, your....er... your rooms are ready for you."

"I will inspect them. Nothing but the best. There are 22 of us. And we are very hungry. We have not eaten since lunch time. Please unload our trunks as quickly as possible. Be careful with them. They contain many treasures from our travels around Europe."

Joseph took charge of the trunks while James showed the Count the rooms. He felt extremely nervous. What if they failed to meet the Count's standards? There were no other rooms available – other than in rival inns. And he was very aware that their owners were all waiting eagerly outside in the street in case things went wrong and they might step in. But, in fact, the Count was quite happy once he was assured that he had the second best room in The Moons.

The Royal party soon took over the entire place. They had clearly enjoyed a drink or two in Portsmouth and were in high spirits as they sang their way through a variety of what James assumed were Russian folksongs. The amount of laughter accompanying them suggested they were very bawdy indeed.

Joseph arranged for the dozen trunks to be unloaded. They were incredibly heavy and, judging by the jangling sound they made, full of metal objects. Gold and silver perhaps? Fortunately the cellar was quite roomy and they eventually managed to fit them in.

Count Kornilov now turned to the serious matter of dinner. He explained that Russians were always hungry – and thirsty – especially when abroad. So what was for dinner? James felt confident about this part as he had a good deal of experience in catering for large numbers of hungry diners. He proudly took the Count through the list of dishes: three ribs of beef, half a sheep, half a lamb, a shoulder of veal, four pullets, four rabbits, a dozen bottles of sack and half a dozen bottles of claret.

The Count pondered for a moment: "Fine, fine…for twenty two Englishmen, but we are Russians! Double it, my good fellow. Double it and it may just be enough." James' smile disappeared. Where on earth would he find as much food again in an hour or two at most? But he dared not admit defeat on this, the biggest occasion he had ever had. This visit would surely go down in history as one of the King's Arms, nay, Godalming's greatest ever events.

He bowed his head and quickly went to find his son.

Joseph prided himself on being able to handle most things: "Leave it to me, father, I'll find the extra food and drink even if I have to go to all the other inns in town. I've garnered a few debts over the years and now is the time to call them in."

James breathed a huge sigh of relief and was just about to check how things were going in the kitchen when Count Kornilov re-appeared : "My friend, we need His Maj... I mean, *Mister* Mikhail's trunk immediately. Where have you put it?"

James Moon explained that all the trunks were in the cellar. How could they tell which one it was? The Count explained it had the initials PM on the top, or possibly the side. Hurry, please!

James Moon went to find his son but then realised he would be away sorting out the food. He looked for his barman, Tom, but saw he was already busy trying to keep up with their guests' thirst. Eventually he found Harry, the farrier, who had managed to stable the horses and the two of them descended the steps into the cellar. By the glow of the lantern they stared through the gloom at the mountain of trunks. If the initials were on the top of the trunk then the chances of seeing them were remote indeed. Harry being the nimbler of the two, began to climb among them while James held the lantern. The task looked hopeless. Then, just when James was trying to work out how best to tell the Count that he couldn't locate the luggage in question, Harry shouted out: "I think I've found it and the good news is, there's only one other trunk on top of it!" With much grunting and swearing they managed to remove it and dragged it up the steps and into the hallway. James looked in at the bar and saw Count Kornilov doing a very odd dance on one of the tables which was creaking ominously. He managed to catch his eye at the end and told him the trunk had been found and brought up from the cellar.

"Oh, don't worry about that, my friend," came the reply rather dismissively. "It's no longer needed. Put it back." James smiled weakly. Mentally he added another charge to the growing bill.

"Is all well, father?" asked his son who had re-appeared and looked very pleased with himself. "I've found the extra supplies and they're now being delivered to the kitchen. It wasn't easy and it wasn't cheap but it's done. But you don't look at all well, father. Perhaps you're overdoing it. Why don't you go and have some rest and I'll see to things." It seemed wise advice.

Thirteen sat down to dinner in the main dining room. Nine made do in one of the bars. Clearly second-tier members of the Grand Embassy. They were all ravenously hungry but their thirst had somewhat abated by now. The whole hotel was filled with the most delicious smells of roast beef (42 lbs), one sheep (56 lbs), three-quarters of a lamb, a shoulder and loin of boiled veal, eight pullets and eight rabbits. And, just in case they were still thirsty, thirty bottles of sack and twelve of claret. A feast fit for a Tsar – or Peter Mikhael - at least.

"Mr Moon," called out the Count. James Moon braced himself. "An excellent feast. Excellent indeed. Now you may leave us to enjoy it. We may carry on for some time as we love to eat. And drink. But don't worry, we will still have an appetite for breakfast!"

As James closed the door to the dining room, he started to breathe heavily. Breakfast! Was there any food at all left for breakfast? He sought out his son.

"Don't worry, father. I have kept some back for breakfast. But surely, even Russians must have their limits?" Surely indeed.

There was little sleep for anyone within half a mile of The King's Arms that night. At one o'clock they seemed to be having a singing contest. At two o'clock, it seemed to be dancing. Three panes of glass fell out of the dining room windows. At four o'clock, a wrestling competition. At five o'clock, some form of shouting contest. But by six o'clock, all was quiet. For one hour and forty three minutes, when a tremendous shout went up: "Breakfast! Breakfast!"

Joseph was ready. With no little foreboding, he looked into the dining room. The curtains were still drawn but the smell of cold roast meat, stale wine, sweaty bodies and more than a dash of vomit was quite overwhelming. Count Kornilov seemed remarkably awake: "My dear friend, we are ravenously hungry. We Russians…"

"Like your food? Yes, Count, we are ready if you would just like to tell me what you want to eat?"

"Let me see… I think we could manage… half a sheep, perhaps just a quarter of lamb, say ten pullets, twelve chickens, several dozen eggs of course, maybe some salad…and to drink…six quarts of wine… mulled wine obviously. And brandy…say three quarts of brandy. Your finest. Yes, that should see us through to our next meal when we reach London."

Joseph nodded. Just what he had anticipated.

Breakfast was altogether a quieter, though not necessarily more sober, an affair. Far less singing and virtually no dancing at all. It was all over by ten thirty.

James was waiting by the coaches as their twenty two Russian guests made their way rather unsteadily to board.

"Our trunks, my friend?"

"All loaded onto the coaches, Count."

"Peter Mikhail asks me to thank you for your warm

hospitality. He has asked me to give you this."

Count Kornilov handed over a large envelope. This was awkward as James had just been about to give him the bill for the stay. Surely the Russians would be generous, would want to create a good impression? James bowed. The Count boarded the coach and they were away. The crowd waved and shouted their goodbyes. The Clacketts sang another song specially composed for the occasion. Charlie Evans was as busy picking pockets as ever.

Joseph was waiting by the main door and James embraced him warmly. What a relief! What a triumph!

"Were they happy with the bill, father? I added a little on for breakages – of which there have been quite a few I can tell you."

"I was just about to hand it to the Count when he gave me this envelope. I'm sure it contains more than enough to cover our costs."

James opened the envelope carefully as he did not wish to tear its precious contents. Inside was a folded piece of paper with what looked like pieces of a Russian newspaper.

"Well, father, what does it say?"

"It says... Thank-you for your warm welcome. Sorry about any damage. Especially the ceiling. Unfortunately we have no funds with us to pay you, but if ever you are in Moscow, please visit and we will return the hospitality."

The two looked at each other. Peter Mikhail had paid not a penny. The cost of the food and the damage was enormous.

"We are ruined," whispered James. "Quite ruined."

"Perhaps not quite," replied Joseph.

"How do you mean?"

"Well, I had heard rumours about our guests and how they seem to make a business of never paying their bills. So I may have forgotten to load all their trunks. So many of them to carry up all those stairs. And so heavy."

"Where are the ones you forgot?"

"Still down in the cellar. Oh, I only forgot the one."

"Not the one with the initials?"

"Perhaps, father."

They quickly made their way down into the cellar. There, in the middle of the floor was the trunk with the initials PM in gold on the side.

"I'm afraid I didn't manage to find the key so I shall have to use a chisel instead."

It was a hefty trunk and took a good few minutes to prise open. Joseph lifted the lid. Inside was an assortment of metal cups and plates and cutlery from all over Europe. They were in reasonable condition but hardly worth a fortune.

"This will barely cover the cost of the breakfast brandy," sobbed a distraught James Moon. "As I thought, we are indeed ruined."

At that moment there was a croaky call from the yard outside.

"Mr Joseph? Are you there?"

"Indeed I am," replied Joseph Moon. "Please come in."

In shuffled Charlie Evans, the town pickpocket. A broad smile spread across his criminal features.

"Didn't do too badly," he smirked. "Not too badly at all. Here, this is your share, Mister Moon."

He handed over a large envelope stuffed with money.

"Thank-you for inviting me to join in the festivities last night. Very decent of you, Mister Moon. The amount they drank made my job quite easy. Best pickings ever. I've split the proceeds in half. Honest. Let me know when you next have royal visitors!"

"That," replied James Moon," will be no day soon."

"A toast," said Joseph Moon. "To Peter Mikhail. Tsar of all the Rooshias. A generous man, even if he doesn't know it!"

Russian Tsar Peter the Great visited Godalming in March 1698 and stayed overnight at the Kings Arms Inn. He and his large entourage caused damage from a wild party but the Tsar had no intention of paying for the stay or the damage.

Humphrey, Jeffrey and Godfrey

THE FURRICIOUS GANG MEET THE POLE CAT

By Martyn Adams

Jeffrey knew he wasn't the tallest of the three teddy bears. He stood over thirty centipedes tall - if he remembered that correctly. Although, come to think of it, they must be quite short centipedes. Maybe it was woodlice? No. He was sure it was centi-somethings. But he was definitely over thirty tall, and that was the important bit. Humphrey was slightly taller being the oldest bear. Godfrey was of course, the shortest because he was the youngest.

Jeffrey also knew that of all the gang, he was the bravest. Unless that is, he got scared or maybe even slightly scared. But then he became the fastest.

And right now Jeffrey was terrified by what he saw.

Now these three bears were known in their home town, as 'The Furricious Gang'. Let me explain the word 'Furricious', it's a word we don't have in our language but animals, particularly bunny rabbits, kittens and teddy bears, do.

When you meet an angry hissing cat - that's ferocious. It might scratch you. When you meet a snarling angry dog - that's ferocious too. It might bite you. But when you tickle a kitten's tummy and it bats its little paws at you and tries to nibble your fingers, that isn't ferocious at all, that's furricious. It's a 'trying-to-be-ferocious-but-not-really' sort of thing.

Likewise when a little puppy jumps on a baby bunny rabbit and they both roll over and start batting at each other with their paws but their eyes are closed and they are really playing, well that's definitely being furricious because no-one gets hurt. At least, no-one is *meant* to get hurt.

But the thing in front of Jeffrey definitely wasn't furricious. It was loud, hungry and angry. It was definitely ferocious and what's more, it was being loud and angry between the Furricious Gang and their home. The three of them had gone for their usual early morning walk but now they were cut off. They couldn't get home to safety without creeping the long way round.

The gang live in a town called Godalming, in Surrey. They live underground through a secret entrance near the bandstand, near the church and close to the river. I can't tell you where exactly, because it's a secret. We have to keep it a secret because if we didn't these three bears would have so many visitors they would soon run out of biscuits, even their chocolate ones, and that would never do.

Besides, dragons think that the word 'furricious' means furry and delicious, so the bears want to stay hidden from *them*. So let's keep it a secret okay?

The little gang stopped and peered around the stone wall. They watched the monster roaring as it ran up and down the field gobbling grass so fast that most of it sprayed up into the air.

"Is it a dragon?" Asked Godfrey, peering from behind Jeffrey.

"No." Said Jeffrey, peering from behind Humphrey. "It's the Grass Muncher. Dragons have wings, breath fire and don't eat grass. It comes here every year, and sometimes during the summer."

"It's a bloody nuisance." Grumbled Humphrey, peering

from behind the stone wall.

They watched it for a minute or two.

"Is it a monster?" Asked Godfrey.

"Yes." Said Jeffrey, because he knew the mostest, or at least he thought he did.

Godfrey sneezed. "Atchoo! Will it eat us?"

"Yes."

"Yuck!" Said Humphrey, flicking a paw and frowning back at Godfrey.

"But it's eating grass..."

"It's very angry. Probably because it can't find teddy bears to eat."

"Do Grass Minchers eat teddy bears?" Godfrey's eyes were filling with tears.

"Yes." Said Jeffrey.

Humphrey sighed. "I wish the bloody council would tell us when they're going to mow the lawn." Humphrey ducked behind the wall. "We're stuck here for a bit."

Jeffrey ducked back beside Humphrey then realised that Godfrey was still staring at the Grass Monster but now he was doing it in plain view. He grabbed him and pulled him back to safety.

Godfrey sneezed again and fell over backwards.

Humphrey, the eldest of the three, seemed a little testy. "Bloody hell Godfrey! Haven't you got a handkerchief?"

"Ye-es." Snivelled Godfrey in a very small, squeaky voice.

"Then use it!"

"I can't."

"Why not?"

"It's at home." He said, very quietly.

Humphrey's eyes flicked skywards for a moment. "Give me strength!"

"So you are going to fight the Grass Monster?" Asked Jeffrey.

"Fight it? Don't be daft! It'd make mincemeat of me."

"I like mincemeat," Said Godfrey remembering his last Christmas party.

Humphrey gave him a dirty look.

"Then why do you need strength?" It seemed to Jeffrey like a logical question and Jeffrey knew he was also the logical-est of the three bears.

"Never mind. We've got to find a place to hide before humans see us."

"We could sneak up on it..."

"Have you ever seen a teddy bear after a grass mower has finished with it?"

"I could make you a sword..."

"Ooh ooh ooh. I like playing swords!" Godfrey started hopping up and down with excitement - just before he sneezed a really strong sneeze and fell over backwards again.

"Godfrey!" The two other bears took out their handkerchiefs and started wiping themselves down.

"I think he's allergic to Grass Munchers." Said Jeffrey.

"You think? Give him your handkerchief before I throw the little cretin to the mower as a small, snot flavoured breakfast snack!" Humphrey sat down and thought hard. "If we weren't so absorbent we could swim along the river, climb up the bank and make a dash for our door when the driver isn't looking."

"We could swim." Suggested Jeffrey.

"Can you swim?"

"Uhm... we can learn, really, really quickly."

"Have you ever seen a soggy teddy bear swim?" Humphrey snarled. "They make a lot of ineffectual splashing as they gradually plummet to the bottom, never to be seen again. Not a pretty sight."

"I like splashing." Offered Godfrey, just before another sneeze sent him flying backwards.

"We could make a submarine, if we could find a pipe and a mirror for a periscope."

"Really?... A submarine. To travel fifty feet. Well at least you don't lack imagina... But wait! We could make a raft. Follow me." Humphrey made a dash from the stone wall to the bank of the river beside the old road bridge.

Jeffrey followed, and Godfrey followed a few seconds later - twice (he sneezed halfway through the first dash).

Now they were hiding behind the cover of the river bank, Humphrey looked around.

"What we need now, is a plank of wood."

"Like that one on the other side of the river?" Jeffrey pointed across the river to a plank of wood.

"Perfect. Except it's in the wrong place."

"I could swim across and get it?" Offered Jeffrey.

"Can you swim?"

"Uhm... I can learn, really, really quickly."

"Have you ever seen a soggy Teddy Bear swim?"

Humphrey snarled. "They make a lot of ineffect... wait a minute." He thought for a moment. "What we need is a shopping bag and string. We could put Godfrey in the bag, float him across the river until he reaches the other side. Then he could tie the string to the plank, float back here and then we can pull the plank over here, climb aboard and paddle down the river."

"Brilliant!" Clapped Jeffrey.

"But we must be very careful. Plastic bags are very dangerous. If a child puts one over his or her head they could suffocate. It's alright for us teddy bears, but not for little children. They mustn't play with plastic bags." Sometimes, Humphrey liked to remind the others that he was the adult and knew adult-type stuff.

So they searched for a plastic bag but they couldn't find one.

"I found some string!" Jeffrey ran up to Humphrey waving something wet and dangly in his paw.

"That's a worm!"

"Oh."

"Besides, mister fluff-for-brains, it's not long enough to cross the river. Even if you stretch it. No. What we need now is a rope."

"Or a pole?" Suggested a voice from behind them. The three bears spun round to see a white cat sitting down and watching them.

"Hello." Said Jeffrey.

"Hello." Whispered Godfrey.

"Who are you?" Asked Humphrey, warily.

"I'm new here. I just moved in. We're neighbours... I think." The cat started licking one of its paws then brushed one of its ears with it. It had a nice red leather collar with a small gold pendant hanging from it.

"Welcome to Godalming, the town where weird things happen in secret. We live down there behind a secret door." Humphrey pointed towards their door. "So don't tell anyone. It's a secret. What's your name?"

"Snowy." She said, smiling in a friendly way and purring a little.

"This is Jeffrey, I'm Humphrey and the snotty one over there is Godfrey. So where do you live?"

Godfrey waved the, now somewhat wetter, handkerchief in greeting and Jeffrey edged towards Humphrey, just in case Godfrey's new handkerchief came too close.

"Over there, under the trees by the tall white pole, near the church."

"Ah. So you must be a Pole Cat?" Suggested Jeffrey.

"Am I? Yes. Yes I suppose I am. Although I'm not sure what the humans do with such a big pole. Do you?"

Humphrey shrugged but Jeffrey, who knew about such matters, explained.

"They do dancing." He said. "Or so I've heard. Every spring, I think. In May... maybe. I read about it. Special dancing. For fertility... I think."

The cat frowned. "Pole dancing?"

"Yes. They're a strange lot, humans. Especially in this town. They hang bits of cloth on the pole and call them flags." Jeffrey added, knowing that that was a real fact and was indeed true. He didn't actually recall seeing anyone pole dancing in Godalming, but anyway sometimes things were far more interesting if they weren't, actually, seen. Like vampires, werewolves, witches and angels. Perhaps they did their pole dancing late at night? Perhaps they danced naked under the moonlight? Who knew? Humans were such strange, scary, creatures.

The cat frowned. "Why do they hang bits of cloth on it?"

"They must have been naughty so the humans string them up as punishment. They used to do that to naughty people and they still do it to their underwear. I've seen it in their gardens. But I have also seen a kind old man sometimes sneak into a garden and rescue the smallest bits of ladies underwear. He's a hero. But apart from him, mostly, they're a weird bunch, them humans."

The cat nodded sagely. Her previous owner, a little old lady, had purchased a little bird in a cage. Snowy naturally assumed it was a packed lunch meant for her owner's favourite feline. She was most surprised when the lady, upon finding the cage empty, Snowy covered in feathers and smiling from ear to ear, got really, really angry.

If her owner had wanted to eat the little morsel herself she should have said so! So Snowy had left home in a huff. She had to agree, humans definitely are a weird lot.

"Will you protect the pole? I think its precious to the humans."

"I don't think so. It's too big for me."

"Oh dear. One would think the humans would look after their poles better, put them all together in one safe place - like a pole vault perhaps; or maybe they could return it from where it came?"

Humphrey slapped his forehead. "Yeh. Right! Return it to Pole-land? That's enough of the puns Jeffrey!"

Jeffrey looked confused while Humphrey turned to the cat.

"We need help Snowy. Can you help us? We need to go home. There is a monster lawn mower outside our door and we need to get past it."

"But I like buns." Whispered Godfrey to Jeffrey not sure why Humphrey had said Jeffrey had had enough of them. He hadn't had any recently, and it was fast approaching the time when they should have finished breakfast. So he started looking for them, between sneezes of course.

"How can I help?" Asked Snowy.

"Well, the current plan is to find some string and a carrier bag. We put Godfrey in the carrier bag and sail him across the river holding one end of the string. Then he gets out of the bag when he reaches the other river bank and ties it to the plank. Then we pull both the plank and Godfrey back here. Then we all jump on the plank and drift down river until we're near our secret front door, then we all jump off and go home without being spotted by the lawn mower man."

Snowy thought for a moment.

"So you need a very long piece of string and a plastic carrier bag with no holes?"

Humphrey nodded.

"… and Godfrey drifts across the river, even though the river current will send him far downstream, and you're sure that absolutely no water will get into the bag and that Godfrey will magically know when to get out?"

Humphrey nodded half a nod then frowned.

"Then, somehow, Godfrey scrambles out of the carrier bag without falling in or losing the bag, and manages to drag the, by now very wet, string and then ties it to the plank - because Godfrey is an expert at tying knots?"

Humphrey looked blank, the gears of his fluff-based brain whizzing round very, very fast ... well, fast for fluff anyway, which really isn't fast at all.

The cat looked across at Godfrey who was now rooting through the long grass looking for buns. He sneezed and did a back flip.

"I think one or two aspects of that plan are not properly thought through. Don't you?" She looked at Humphrey sideways.

Humphrey sat down heavily on the grass.

"You're right. Godfrey doesn't know how to tie knots." He said.

"Besides," suggested Snowy, "Wouldn't it be easier just to cross the bridge?"

"Brilliant!" Humphrey shot to his feet. "I should send Godfrey over the bridge."

The cat covered her eyes in exasperation.

"No. No. No. You ALL cross the bridge, launch the plank, jump on it and drift down river."

Humphrey though for a moment.

"Even better. Yes! Why didn't I think of that? Godfrey! Jeffrey! Come here."

"Something to do with having fluff-for-brains?" She suggested, but quietly to herself so that they couldn't hear.

They made a dash across the bridge and appeared on the other side.

"Jeffrey, you grab one end and I'll grab the other." Said Humphrey.

Snowy called out "Don't forget..."

They lifted the plank. "One, two, threeeeeee..." Yelled

Humphrey

"...to think it..."

The plank struck the water with an enormous splash and quickly moved to the middle of the river before lazily drifting away.

"...through first." Snowy sighed, closed her eyes and shook her head.

Jeffrey looked at Humphrey's dismayed expression. "I think your plan was better. One should never trust the plans of a pole cat."

Humphrey nodded in agreement.

"Besides," explained Jeffrey "there might be alligators in the river. Perhaps we could make a submarine now? If we can find a pipe and a mirror for a periscope."

Humphrey spotted Godfrey, he was grinning from ear-to-ear and holding up a shopping bag.

"Well done Godfrey! Too late as usual, but well done anyway."

Godfrey dived inside the bag to search for buns. He didn't find any.

Humphrey clapped his paws. "That gives me an idea!"

"What?" Asked Jeffrey.

"We'll wear shopping bags over our heads as a disguise!"

Godfrey, now with the bag over his head and unable to see, was staggering round and round in circles - until he sneezed.

"But not that one." Suggested Jeffrey.

"Snowy!" Humphrey called out. "Can you find us two more shopping bags?"

"Any particular colour?" She asked sarcastically.

"Any colour will do."

"Red please!" Called out Jeffrey.

"With some buns in?" Squeaked Godfrey, disappointed that he'd missed out on a treat earlier.

Snowy set off, not really intending to find any discarded bags. She just wanted to be away from these idiotic bears. Perhaps she could scrounge a breakfast from a human. She idly imagined a golden fish swimming in a bowl of milk, with maybe a cream topping and a little catnip on the side.

The Furricious Gang dragged their shopping bag back across the bridge to the river bank and waited for Snowy to return. After ten minutes, which is a very long time for teddy bears, Humphrey decided that one of them should set off to find more shopping bags so that each of them would have their own disguise.

As Godfrey had effectively made the inside of the bag his, what with the sneezing and all, he was volunteered to do the finding. So, wearing his disguise over his head, Godfrey set off along the path, past the church and into the grave yard.

What Humphrey quickly realised is that poor little Godfrey couldn't see where he was going. He kept banging into things, like gravestones and the wall, and he kept walking round in circles. In the end Humphrey ran up and stopped him.

"What we need is..."

Just then Snowy appeared dragging two new carrier bags. "Don't ask me how or why. But I happened to find these. I thought they might be able to help."

"Brilliant! But I think we might have a problem." Said

Humphrey. "Plastic bags like these are dangerous to children, they must have air holes - and we can't see out of them anyway."

"Come here." Sighed Snowy, and she went to each one in turn and using her sharp claws she made big airy eye holes so that they could see out.

So Humphrey thanked her and invited her around to tea one day at their secret home. Then, safely wearing their new disguises, the three bears walked the long way home up to Church Street, along the paths to Great George Street and then back down the path to the Bowling Club. They managed this without being spotted, or eaten, by the Grass Muncher; but mainly because the driver had stopped some time ago and had nipped into the high street for breakfast at the Godalming Cafe.

So, if you happen to be in Godalming early one morning and see three upside-down shopping bags strolling down the high street, you'll know it's probably the Furricious Gang out for a walk. Please don't lift the bags off the bears though, there might be a dragon watching and dragon's think teddy bears are furry and delicious.

However, if you see a white cat with a red collar, then do wave hello. It might be Godalming's very own special pole cat.

...and if you happen to visit a certain place in Godalming at the bewitching hour in the middle of the night during the Spring Equinox on a leap year, you might just see the humans of Godalming pole dancing.

The Tsar's phantom is said to reside at the Kings Arms and manifests itself by kicking off its boots between 1 o'clock and 2 o'clock in the morning.

NO SUCH THING AS TIME

By Judy Coleman

In a pool of sunlight the shadow marking time fell across the sundial's face. The shadow followed its slow, daily pattern around the warm circle of hours… but just then, the shadow shuddered… and so did time.

The sundial lazed in a small back garden close to Farncombe narrowboats moored in the midday sun. Here the silver-haired figure of Mark Quaint shuffled into his garden.

"Good day to you, one and all," he announced as he admired the boats, swans, ducks and the flowing River Wey.

However, clocks were his real passion and he continued on his way to examine his sundial, as he did each day. He liked to imagine the Earth spinning slowly, casting a small time-shadow on the old pocked surface. It should be noon exactly.

Well-known for his lectures on clocks and the measurement of time through history, Quaint had many clock collections. They roosted all over his house; huge round faced owl-clocks, tall ornate grandfather clocks and wall clocks. Some clocks had cuckoos leaping out to surprise his visitors. The clocks kept him unusually busy in his old age. A lot of clocks had solid brass keys to wind up their metal ticking. Pendulum clocks needed weights pulling down at regular intervals. His precious clocks of historic value filled his locked garage, stacked and packed to the rafters. They needed dusting and oiling.

Each hour, and half hour, the house shook with

chimes, booms, bongs, tinkles, and alarmed cuckoos. Different sounds of ticking pattered from all corners like scampering mice; soft chatterings, melodious tickings, hurried clatters and metallic whirs. The ticking percussion permeated the scent of polish, wood, metal, and old carpets; all the clocks talking at once, conversing to each other through the dim lit interior.

In the garden Mark Quaint peered at the sundial. His glasses, perched low on his nose, jumped as he adjusted them in surprise. He moved closer to inspect the face of the sun-dial.

"Three O'clock!... Impossible!" he snorted. "My watch did say twelve noon exactly. As did the house clocks. The sundial must be fast - out of step with – time. But that's an impossibility." He moved his hands feeling for faults down the ivy festooned pedestal and tested its base. "Perfectly firm. The pedestal hasn't shifted."

Standing upright was another surprise, for as he heaved up from his crouch it was all too easy, he felt like a boy again. Usually scrambling to his feet made him breathless, yet just now it was as if years had peeled away from his old body.

He glared at his petrified, white faced watch and listened to its conscientious workings. "As a scientist and clock specialist," he addressed the garden and trees, waving his astonished arms, as if giving a lecture. "I have to believe in the sundial, yet, never in forty years has my watch been out of sync with the sundial. They are always spot on. Spot on the dot of Greenwich Time. Except of course, when the time change occurs from winter to summer time. And this is always very inconvenient for me, I have so many clocks. Meanwhile I'll settle this problem and check with the speaking clock. Excuse me!"

He started with a grunt to climb the garden steps - but with a wide grin, and without effort he strode up - two at a time. He played hopscotch on his crazy paving and almost forgot 'time'. He did a tap dance too. Then became embarrassed in case a boat might pass and adjusted himself into the distinguished person he hoped he was.

"This won't do. The world had become a very strange planet indeed. A Walt Disney Oddity! Suddenly it's so easy to play! My childhood is back, whether I like it or not. But I think I like it!"

"No! Now let me think? This could be serious. Losing track of time. These symptoms can occur at my age. Hallucinations. Must check with the Mill Doctors. Too much time alive. That's what's wrong … Time! … Time, I've lived too long. Can't be well." Yet he felt exceedingly well. A lightness enveloped him like a champagne intoxication, even though he hadn't had a drop all week!

At last Quaint's elegant foxtrot gait took him inside his busy tick-tocking home. He stopped confounded. His orchestra of clock music sounded alien.

The grandfather clock, the concert conductor halfway up the stairs had lost its consistent time tapping pace … it was slurred and slow. The grandmother clock whose feminine chatter in the tempo of metronome precision was ticking with an irregular pulse, her arms stuck out at a quarter past twelve. - Like Jesus on the cross. In contrast, the wound up clocks were whirring, unwinding, rushing in a race to early exhaustion. Their metal innards useless. "My lovelies, my beautiful clocks. Don't give up. We'll sort this." He uttered in haste.

Quaint's overweight, orange spaniel Ticker, eased herself from her blanketed basket into an immaculate summer-salt, and landed on flatfooted paws barking staccato yelps of excitement.

"Shhh, Ticker. Listen. What's happened to us? What's going on?"

Ticker shook herself, then jumped as high as the ceiling, pleased to see him. Mighty pleased with herself too!

He observed her in astonishment – then an enormous thought occurred to him. "You've become light, just like me! That's it. By heaven - its gravity. Gravity's gone! Watch me!" He jumped in the air. If his hands hadn't been ready to catch his upward bounce, his head would have gone straight through the ceiling.

"Gravity's gone! Gravity's gone." He dropped down, light footed, a gymnast. "Einstein's famous theory has gone haywire! Gravity, the ruler of the Universe. My word, this is shocking! Do you agree Ticker? We're light as feathers. The pendulum clock weights have become light too, and can't keep their wheels turning. The clocks are stopping. Goodness - **The Sundial** - that's the clue. The Sundial was right. It showed the time variation with my watch - the Earth must be spinning faster. We'll be thrown off by centrifugal force! Do you understand Ticker. It's as if we're on a roundabout and being flung off!"

The old man with his shock of white hair which now stood on end escaping gravity too, ran outside. He leapt the eight steps and over-shot the sundial. The sun was at a low angle. The sundial's time shadow lay with a sinister smirk at four o'clock on its hot face. It revealed even more time difference. Earth Time was now - - four hours fast!

In his house, the television burst into life with a hiss and blur of a disconnected aerial. The image was faint, but Mark Quaint made out an announcer.

"Scientists confirm the Earth's atmosphere was caught in the tail end of Comet Spinal. The friction has acted on Earth's turning speed with the effect of a whip on a spinning top. Scientists report the Earth is marginally out of control, the spinning will increase speed for another ten hours. They hope, they… think, it will normalise.

Meanwhile populations in the south of England should move northwards as sea-levels are rising due to oceans gravitating by the spinning forces to the equator and flooding outwards. Flooding will be wide-spread especially along river valleys. Travellers should only take essential belongings. There is no time left."

While she was speaking, the announcer had started to grip the desk, her papers were lifting. Her legs were lifting. She clung on to keep her head in view, and when her skirts slid over her face the screen went blank.

Quaint stared at his clocks. There was no such thing as clock-time any more. Not their time. Would it ever be the same again? Multiples of solemn faces stared back.

"Please keep safe. Ticker and I have to go north. I hope it will get better for us." He picked up his favourite owl clock and another wooden cat curled round her frightened 'time face' and with a gentle pat, placed them both in his green washing-up bowl. If the sea came in they might rise with the tide.

"The owl and the pussy-cat went to sea in a beautiful pea-green boat," he hummed trying not to alarm them.

"Come with me Ticker," he bellowed at Ticker waiting for her midday walk. Already the narrowboats were straining at their moorings. "Jump Ticker," roared Quaint.

… It was easy. Up and over the road into the sky, over the Lammas Lands, and above Waitrose, above the cranes building new houses and apartments. Above the steeples of St Peter and St Paul. They landed and jumped, up they went again over the elaborate spires and towers of Charterhouse School. The boys were playing a football match in the sky. It was a Harry Potter scene for real, even the referee was floating. They were out of control chasing a fly-away ball.

Below, they saw the river and railway line trace separate

routes through the small town of Godalming, so very far below in the fast fading light. Quaint saw Ticker had her dinner-dish and spoon, of all things! They were child and puppy again. Excited!

The enormous red moon was on the horizon rising at a visible rate. Animals and people were leaping in a northward direction. A black and white cow from the Lammas Lands jumped straight over the moon.

"Hey diddle-diddle - race from Earth's middle,

The cow jumped over the moon.

The little dog laughed to see such fun

And her dish ran away with its spoon."

Sang Mark Quaint as Ticker's dinner-dish floated off into the crimson sky.

The Earth sang too... humming like a huge spinning top.

Godalming's Public Bath called the 'Ginny' was on the River Wey near Hell's Ditch below Charterhouse School. There were also a swimming pool in Charterhouse School for its students.

ARRIVAL

By Stefan Kuegler

I wiped my eyes. I was shattered. We were all shattered. Thirty-six hours travel using many modes of transport to arrive at this point.

It was freezing. The snow lay on the ground inches thick. What was I doing here? I could see the same question on the expression of my family. Those 36 hours before, we had been experiencing warm, sunny 29°C whereas now we were boot deep in snow and I couldn't feel my hands.

What were we thinking?

The start of a new adventure. I didn't expect this. None of us expected this.

"Where are we staying?" My wife asked, shivering.

"Somewhere warm hopefully." I replied.

"Did we really want to do this?"

I shrugged, we had made the plan and executed it. We were in England. It was great. Sort of. Maybe it will get warmer. What a complete change from Sydney, Australia. We had already been asked a few times - were we thinking right? Moving from Sydney to England. Most people moved the other way. Why did you do it?

Why? It was the question that was going through both my and my wife's mind. The kids were excited by the snow. They had never seen it before. My daughter wasn't sure whether to touch it or not.

"What is this?" my daughter had asked when she first saw it. She was three years old, short curly hair hidden under a pink beany. She was dressed in the thickest coat that we could find in Australia, not thick enough for here. She had already mentioned that it was cold when we walked out of the station.

I felt tired.

"The last leg." My wife sighed, as if reading my mind. She was tired as well. She stood near the luggage that we had pulled around since we had landed in Heathrow. It hadn't seemed so heavy when we first started on the journey.

"The last leg." I nodded. I moved over and gave her a hug. The kids joined in. If nothing else the trip had galvanised us as a family. Not that we weren't beforehand but a trip like this can either pull you apart or you can pull together to become even closer - some shaky times but it had mostly been good. It is amazing what you learn about yourselves in two days of close contact.

The last leg indeed. We had started the trip eight time zones earlier, flying out of Sydney for an unseen destination.

Godalming. It was only a name on the map. The website looked good. It had all the things we wanted. It looked sunny. It looked inviting. Looking around the train station now, it didn't match the pictures I remembered.

We had started with a long haul flight to Singapore – ten hours in economy class with two kids snuggled between us. The constant wriggling to get comfortable. Me, not the kids. I'm over six foot tall and so the seat can be a little tight. There is only so long you can sit with your legs stretched out in awkward angles. The kids were fine. They even curled up on the chairs and slept. Lucky buggers. I looked in envy at them for most of the trip. I looked at the people in business class in the same way.

Then another long haul flight to Heathrow. Only three

hours stop-over in Singapore, enough time to stretch legs, go to the toilet without have to touch the walls to stand upright, and look at all the shops with the bottles, clothes, perfumes, toys. We had nothing that we wanted to buy. Well that's not quite right, we had no room for anything so there was no point looking. We looked anyway. Before long it was time to board the plane again. Not even time to get bored.

A long wait in Heathrow to get through border control. It was nearly long enough to make us want to turn around and board the next plane back. We finally got through. Everyone was friendly, at least.

We had planned our trip so we knew that we had to catch the train into Paddington, subway and then train out to Godalming. Another four hours. Could we stand it? There was a real risk that we would fall asleep on the train and miss our stop. We didn't know what we were looking for or which stop came before what. We might know the name but it was just as foreign as if it had been in Brazil.

"Stop running."

"I'm not. I just want to get there."

"It's not a race."

It had been a running joke. I was speeding ahead with two of the suitcase while the others trailed in my dust. I walked fast but didn't realise that I walked that fast. I had travelled alone a lot so I always wanted to get to the hotel and relax. The flights were hard enough so I wanted to stretch out. One of the drawbacks of being so tall – needed lots of leg room to be comfortable.

It meant that when I got going, I was quickly outpacing everyone. I had to check to see if they were still behind me otherwise they might have got lost. I had the map in my head. I moved on instinct. I still do.

Get to the train and then rest. Get to the next, keep going till the next rest spot. It was how I travelled. It worked for me. Not for those travelling with me.

It hadn't been commuter time so the subway and trains were not so busy. It was early morning and we missed most of the commuters or we were heading in the opposite direction. We had never seen so many people. Sydney has a few but London was another step up again. I had been to India but I wasn't expecting this. With two suitcases, you were quite wide so you needed to navigate well in order to miss the people otherwise you might end up carrying a few with you. The suitcases were heavy enough without needing more weight.

The last train trip through the Surrey countryside had been lovely. We hadn't really decided how long we were staying but it would be for at least two years. The countryside was not as I pictured it. The greenery was missing. It was a magical white instead.

I had picked up a local paper on the train. Heaviest snow for December in a long time. Just our luck. It would be lovely when we found a place and could enjoy it. We hadn't expected a white Christmas but it might be what we were getting. Now it seemed to stretch on in the distance, covering everything with a brilliant white but making it very cold as well. The cold was penetrating our clothes. I couldn't feel my fingers or the tip of my nose.

"Why did we decide to do this?" I thought again as we trudged through the snow. I couldn't feel my toes either.

We had needed a change. We needed something new. We needed a new adventure. Well, looking out the window we certainly had a new adventure. Probably more than we bargained for.

Sun for Snow.

Was that a fair exchange? At the moment it didn't seem

like it. Thinking back only a few days ago the temperature was 40°C, you can see that this might have been a bit of a culture shock. In more ways than one. I hadn't expected snow. It was so white. It was a lovely sight. I had never seen such a glorious white. The icicles as they hung from the trees. The bare leafless trees covered with a lite dusting of snow that shone in the morning sun.

There was sun but it had little warmth. But when it hit the icicles just so, the prism of light and colours was the most extraordinary thing you could wish to see. You'd never see something like that in Sydney. The icicles held your attention as the colours danced within the light. I could start to see the beauty of the snow.

But when you're cold and hungry and very tired, there is only so much that beauty can make you feel.

"Do we look for the place or what?" I asked. I wanted to know how everyone was feeling before my hands gripped the suitcase handles and started walking.

"I think we need food."

"I'm hungry." My son, even though he is only five, already has the appetite of a much larger boy. I can't blame him today, I'm feeling quite peckish myself.

"I'm cold." My daughter is very thin and there is hardly any fat on her. She is a string-bean. The coat must be doing very little to keep her warm. The thrill of the snow was going as hands started to freeze.

"I'll see if I can find anything." My wife rummaged around in one of the suitcases, finding a few items until another jumper is forth-coming. The look on my daughter's face said enough.

"It's this or be cold." I could see her thinking about it. My wife quickly stepped in.

"It'll be under your coat. No-one will see it." That

seemed to be make it less painful and more bearable.

What is it with children?

"It's cold." My daughter complained as she took off a few items to add the new layer. Of course, it's cold. You're taking somethings off to add something more. A little pain for, hopefully, a lot of gain. Maybe a bit. Nope, don't see it like that. Just see it as pain. A pain to put clothes on. A pain to take clothes off. If we were being truthful, then it was a pain to be in this cold country. I could hear the thoughts going round in my daughter's head. So far neither of our kids had said anything. It was still to come. I was certain.

"Better?"

Just a nod, better than anything else at this stage. I'm still tired.

"Ready?" I looked at my exhausted family. My daughter looking like a puff ball with all her layers on. My son, yawning, but nodded, ready to continue. He has been a trouper so far. Never flagging and somehow managing to keep up with my hectic pace, even though his legs are half my size. And my wife, smiling as always, keeping us all happy and rugged up.

"Maybe a little slower. It would be good to see the town where we might be living."

"True." I looked around the train station. There didn't seem to be an obvious direction in which the town lay. Two signs, both talking about the High street, pointing in different direction. I hoped that one way was as good as another.

I dragged the suitcases behind me, very conscious of the noise they were making. I was already tired (had I mentioned that?) and I had no idea where I was going. I was waiting for the likely question. It didn't come. I looked behind me. Everyone was trudging through the snow. It was a new experience. The only thing that I was really aware of was that suitcases don't really roll well on snowy roads.

I continued to pull them along. Both arms started to ache. It was heavy work.

"It's cold."

I looked back at my daughter. She was three as I said so she always had some words of wisdom. This time she was spot on.

"It is cold." I half turned as I spoke. She was good, walking behind me, watching the suitcases in case they stepped out of line.

"Where are we going?" She asked after a moment's thought.

"We are trying to find our hotel."

"Where is it?"

"In the town somewhere."

"Where?"

I was starting to lose patience. I had little to start with. The trip had taken everything from me. I was just on remote. If I needed to do more than the basics it was going to be tough. I just wanted to find where we were staying and then ignore everything for a few hours while I turned back into a human being.

"Somewhere. I don't know. Remember. I haven't been here before either."

She just nodded. I could tell that she wasn't happy with that answer but unfortunately it was the best I could do.

"Stop. Road." I was also starting to avoid full sentences. My daughter stopped and waited. My son nearly ran the back of her and then my wife stopped behind them.

"Okay, stick with us." I waited for a moment, now really thinking that the likelihood of cars in this weather was probably unlikely but nevertheless I was unaccustomed to this so I just did what I knew best.

"Okay, let's go." I started dragging the suitcases again.

"The Red Lion." I pointed with my chin.

"What is that?"

"Pub."

"Is that our hotel?" My daughter was obviously tired. She didn't want to say it but she was making it known that she wanted to stop.

"No. Still a little to go." I really didn't know how far it was. I knew it was in the centre of the town where we were going but I didn't know whether we were close or not. I didn't want to get her hopes up yet. I was looking forward to it as well.

We stepped out onto the main road. The rows of building formed a corridor that rolled off in the distance. The white of the snow gave it a majestic look. Two furrows through the snow marked where the cars had driven. It was a weird scene and couldn't really compute it in my mind.

"How it's look?" My wife asked as she came up behind me.

"Picturesque." It was the only way to describe. It might not be the most picturesque street but it had a feeling about it. It felt inviting. There was a warm about how the town looked. We had landed on our feet here.

"I'm sure it looks better without the snow as well."

I wasn't sure. The snowy landscape somehow added a postcard feel. It just needed a horse-drawn sleigh to pass us by for the image to be complete. In my mind's eye I could image the warm fire and the cosy blankets that would soon envelop us and drive the cold away from us.

"Let's keep moving. I can't feel my feet."

I must admit my toes were also quite cold and maybe there was a better time to admire the view than now. I started to move down the street, still dragging the suitcases. I would be happy to deposit them in the room. I would soon deposit them in any spare space. They contained everything we owned. Mostly clothes for the time being until the rest of our stuff arrived. I shivered again.

It was cold. I continued on through the snow. I felt like I was in Alaska or Canada, walking down the street of a sleeping snowed-in town. I looked at the names of the shops as we walked down the street. They were open. It seemed strange to me that even with the snow the town was still alive. On every show I had ever seen I thought snow brought places to a standstill.

"Chemist." I pointed again with my head to Boots as we passed it. The blast of heat that escaped the shop as the automatic doors opened reminded that there was heat in the village somewhere. It was a welcome feeling for the instance that it warmed my face.

"Ohhh." My daughter seemed to enjoy it as well.

"Nice, huh?"

She stopped for a moment as the doors stayed open, savouring the heat.

"Let's keep going." I prompted, we were blocking the way into the store.

The heat had been a nice interlude but we needed to

find our place. We kept on walking. Our eyes were wide. Or at least wide-ish due to lack of sleep. The shop names we didn't recognised although we could see what they were. The same as home. Clothes. More chemists. Cafés. Charity shops.

That was new. Charity shops. Interesting notion but no time to look. People were getting grumpy – we already looked like the four dwarves, didn't need to act like them.

"Are we there yet? I can't feel my feet." My wife called forward to me. I shrugged.

I kept on trudging on. The street, the High Street of Godalming, continued on, white and straight. Various sights and scenes drifted past as well as the occasional snow flurry.

"I see it." I called over my shoulder as the sign for the Hotel came into view. Kings Arms and Royal Hotel. Strange name but it had looked friendly on the Internet.

"Finally." That was the expression of a person at the end of their strength. And probably their patience. And their food reverses. I continued to pull our suitcases, thinking of the warm interior and a comfortable chair in which to rest my weary body. The problem would happen when I would want to get up again.

"Let's just have a sit down inside first." I stop for a second at the entrance. "Large columns." I walk through and push open the door. I greeted by a warm embrace. The heat from the hotel is enough to defrost my feelings of home. I am nearly trampled by my family as they rushed to be in the warmth of the Hotel as well. I pushed forward and make room for them. I pulled the cases into the main foyer, place them out of the way.

"Let's have a drink."

Drinks ordered – hot chocolates all round. Food was

also ordered but it would come a little later. For the moment we can wrap our hands around the cups – circulation comes back to our hands – and the heat of the drink heating our insides. We can finally appreciate the surroundings and the town. We look at some of the old pictures on the walls, showing the town at various times. It was a world away from what he had left behind.

"That feels better." My hands were thawing out. I pulled the suitcases close and started to check them, making sure they were all there. it was a habit rather than any real need.

"Where are we?"

"Godalming." I tried to pronounce the name but I think I failed. It was unlike any name I had heard before.

"Where's that?" My daughter asked.

I stopped for a moment to try and understand what my 3 year old might be thinking.

"What do you mean?"

"Are we still in Australia?"

"No, we are now in England." As I said those words, I knew that it was true. The immortal words from 'Wizard of Oz' came to me and they were just as relevant – we certainly weren't in Kansas anymore. I didn't know what to feel. There was an excitement of starting a new adventure and then the strangeness of everything and wanting to be back where we belonged. We were certainly out of our comfort zone.

I smiled across at my wife. She rested her head on the chair and she nearly looked like she was asleep. I couldn't blame her. I was feeling exhausted. I looked at my watch. It was still early.

"Should we have a walk around the town?"

There were shrugs all round. Everyone was happy within the warmth of the hotel and there seemed to be little inclination to move at this point.

"In a little while." My wife voiced what everyone was thinking. "Another drink first?" She held up her empty cup.

I nodded. I was tired but I also knew that sleeping now would be the worst thing to do. At the same time it was the only thing I wanted to do. Curl up in a warm bed and let sleep take me.

We sat in silence, probably looking a little stunned.

"I really need a shower." I had been smelling something, and belatedly I realised that it was me. After 24 hours in the airplane and then a further four hours travelling around on the train, there was an odour that was following me.

My wife nodded, too exhausted to speak.

"I'll check in and see if we can get into our room." I went to the front desk. After a quick conversation about where we were from, and then the question about why did we come to Britain from that sunny Isle, to which I didn't have a ready answer, we were shown to our room. It was large enough for the four of us. Everybody fell onto their beds or someone else's bed.

We all quickly changed and showered. That helped us feel human again and we were ready to step out into this new world. We all looked at each other and then left the room.

We stepped out the front of the hotel. Left or right? It was all new so either direction would be interesting. I held my hands out looking for inspiration.

"Right."

We walked slowly, trying to take everything in. While nothing was so different that we didn't understand what it was, there were other differences that were subtle that made us look twice before we were sure what we were looking at. We walked past the stores – recognising none of the names.

We visited a few estate agents trying to get an understanding of the place and what homes might be available in the future. It is friendly and welcoming – it is a comfort as we make our way along the cold street. The snow lying in the street gives a clean, crisp feeling underfoot. The town is covered just enough it to make it appear like a Christmas card.

We are wrapped against the cold, snow is falling. We stop for a while in the street to take in the scene. Nothing like this would ever occur in Australia. Standing there, feeling the wonder of the snow, the bite of the cold wind upon our faces, we realise that a new adventure has started. The old life of heat, sun and the sameness that you can experience when you have stayed somewhere too long have been replaced by cold, snow and newness. A world ready to be explored. A new place to call home, to grow as a family and to have fun.

THE TALE OF THE MIRROR

By Heather Wright

The house in Godalming looked derelict when we first saw it. Seven thousand tiles were missing from the roof, it had no floors and we viewed by balancing precariously along ancient but very substantial joists. Some were rotten as the whole building was riddled with dry rot, wet rot and woodworm not to mention death-watch beetle.

It needed re-wiring and re-plumbing and had been thoroughly vandalised. Neither a hook nor a doorknob remained. It was a shell, a beautiful, magnificent and challenging shell, dating back to the 15th Century and steeped in history.

The garden was totally overgrown to the extent that you couldn't tell whether there were flower beds, shrubberies, paths, low walls or any other features though we did discover a well which we later learned, dated back to the 18th Century. It was a large round waterhole surrounded by a crumbling brick wall that was covered in Ivy. An enormous area outside the dilapidated and decaying conservatory was totally taken over by Cotoneaster, the fierce red berries daring you to challenge its presence. One almost expected a handsome prince to come slashing his way through the undergrowth to find the sleeping beauty. No such luck, though there were plenty of frogs about!

Shutters hung from the windows. A shed door banged and clattered in the wind. The river, running the length of the garden, was so strangled by overgrown river plants and weeds that you could almost hear it choking as it struggled to make its way to the Thames.

We stood in the driveway within a walled garden of some considerable size. The rotting gates through which we had originally entered were behind us and it was as if we were within another world.

"Who would have thought there was such a magnificent house behind those rotting gates," said John.

"It may have been magnificent at one time" I replied "but it certainly looks neglected and unloved to my inexperienced eye".

"Yes, but you and I together darling could make this house beautiful". This was a statement often referred to in subsequent years while "darling" got on with it and the Lord of the Manor made a landing stage in the river.

So we bought it. Everyone thought we were mad but what perfect foil for someone with an adventurous spirit; and we both had one of those!

We lived, for about four months in a small caravan in the garden, lent to us by John's sister and her husband. Indeed, if they hadn't needed it at the end of that time we would have been there for a lot longer but they needed a holiday with their young family and our time was up. It was no joke with two teenage boys and a new kitten. We had to put the beds up before we could make a cup of tea in the mornings, the kitten ran up and down everything he could see whether it was legs, curtains or trees and every time John and I turned over in bed at night one teenager or the other would say "Aye Aye!"

During this time we had the pest control people in, roofers, tilers, electricians, plumbers and even a craftsman brought out of retirement to restore the rubbed brick arches over the windows which had been agreed because the house was a Grade 11 listed building.

And what did we have then? We had a house that had a roof, floors and central heating. We had toilets that flushed and light switches and plugs that worked. No more did the letters go through the letter box and straight into the cellar....but it was still not really habitable. It needed preparing for decorating throughout, the actual papering and painting would be a doddle compared to the heavy task of preparation. The first priority had to be fitting a kitchen and money was getting short. All that was left in the kitchen was a really useful fitted dresser which, cleaned out and painted, provided plenty of storage for crockery. There was also a pantry, which was previously a back staircase I understand, and needed quite a bit of TLC but then was really useful. So we went to Solarbo which in the 1970's was a "do it yourself" dream for those who were gluttons for punishment or really loved DIY. We thus eventually had a pine farmhouse style kitchen with a huge table made specially to fill the centre of the room. We had, by then, totally run out of money and could only progress at the rate of what could be spared from our joint monthly income. So it took a while.

I recall when the caravan had to be returned, manically painting one bedroom in temporary white and scrubbing the floor in order to make it reasonably acceptable to move into. We then put in bunk beds and our bed and the four of us camped in that room until I could get the next one reasonable habitable. I was horrified. I thought it was terrible all of us sleeping in one room yet it was at least six times as big as the caravan and we didn't have to move the beds to make the tea! The perk was that we didn't have a kitten running all over us in the night.

We loved it though. The boys liked living near to their friends and close to the teenage life of Godalming having been out in the sticks for so long. They enjoyed being able to get around independently and loved the small boat John had bought to go with his landing stage! An outboard motor was another priority and we were all set up for trips up the river.

They say that in your forties you should change your husband, your house or your job. We had both just changed our jobs and the adventure of the house was a real commitment to each other and the future, a commitment that went on long after my husband died just eight years later.

Just outside the back door there was a yard with a crumbling brick outhouse and cracked concrete floor. This had its own gate out into the garden, very close to the river.

Things came down the river.

John loved things. He was a collector of all things large, small and indifferent, valuable and useless. So the back yard, thankfully concealed from any visitors was full of things that mainly came down the river. For instance, as narrow boats were moored close by on various parts of the bank and the boat house was nearby we had, at a count, fifteen mops that had fallen off the boats and floated down river into our part and had perhaps got tangled in the weeds. There were a few garden seats that had been thrown in by vandals though we rang the council to have those returned most of the time. Bric a brac of all kinds graced the yard and my influence was totally redundant when it came to pleas to tidy it up. It was his yard and he was Steptoe!

The house had a character of its own. It wrapped itself around us and absorbed our personalities into its ambience. Maybe it was gratitude for being hauled back from dereliction and being lovingly if not lavishly, restored. Maybe it was our contentment that made us feel that way. In any event we came to consult it on many things like what colour to put on the walls for instance. I would buy little match pots of paint and daub here and there in the room designated for decoration and wait to see which one it wanted. Fanciful, you might say, but it worked for me. We always felt comfortable about the choices we eventually made. We loved coming home as we always felt a warm welcome and a feeling of well-being in a way we never had before and were almost childishly thrilled by any small task that had been successfully completed.

However, it was not always good vibes we received!

To furnish our new home appropriately we spent a lot of time at the auctions. We usually went together which was mainly successful, but there were times when John went alone and came back with an item I had my doubts about. Sometimes it went into a shed and was returned to the next auction where it frequently fetched twice as much as he paid for it and other times it hung around for a while and then we lost on the deal. One day John came home with a huge mantle mirror. It had a sculpted gold frame with tapestry panels and when we investigated the backing, it was packed with newspapers reporting the latest escapades of Lily Langtry. It was beautiful.

"Where had you thought of putting it?" I asked.

"I'm not sure"

"You must have had some idea where it would go when you bid for it" I said with a sigh. I loved it but had no vision of where it might go either.

"Well yes, I thought it could look good on the landing. What do you think shall we try it there?" He looked at me for a reaction.

"Fine". I said. That was what I always said if I wanted to sound reasonable when really I was full of doubts.

We had a very large landing which was probably planned that way to keep down the size of the bedrooms for heating purposes. It was the size of a fairly large bedroom and we had an antique refectory table c1756 against the back wall and opposite the window. It seemed like a good place as it would reflect the light from the window. John rested the mirror on the table, upright, to see what it looked like and how we felt about it. We left it and went downstairs for supper.

That was when it started.

It was unbelievable. The atmosphere in the house changed. There were shadows where there had been no shadows. The air was cold. It was chill everywhere but particularly on the landing. Warm and comforting became cold and threatening making the hair on the back of my neck constantly prickle. I kept feeling the need to look behind me as though there was someone there. I shivered repeatedly on the warmest day.

Crazy! I thought at first that I must be imagining it but soon realised that this was not the case. Even reflections in the mirror seemed distorted. I felt that if I said too much John would just laugh so I needed to wait until he said something.

He was out that evening and up in London the next day. The boys made no comment though they were not around much either. I couldn't stand it and the next evening had to broach the subject.

"What do you think about the mirror on the landing then, do you think it feels right......er, looks right?"

"Well", he replied "I know it sounds silly, a bit like you and your paint blobs, but I don't think the house likes it".

My relief must have been obvious but I replied casually;

"What shall we do then, take it to the next auction or try it somewhere else. Perhaps it just isn't right in that particular place; after all, they say that if there are spirits in a house they are most likely to be on the landing".

"Spirits....rubbish" laughed my sceptical husband "

OK, let's try it somewhere else."

We put it in the morning room over the recently restored Victorian fireplace. It fitted exactly to the width of the marble mantelpiece.

"Don't know why we didn't put it here first" John said "seems pretty obvious to me to put a mantle mirror over a fireplace."

He was right. The mirror looked superb above the white marble and reflected the trees in the front garden with no distortion at all.

"Let's leave it over the weekend before we fix it "I said cautiously. We could do it next week.

Calm returned to our home.

Over twenty years later, when selling the house twelve years after John had died, I was asked what fixtures would be included and were there any that I wished to sell. The only item I put a price on was the mirror and that was accepted which was a good thing as I really couldn't have moved it from its perfect and possibly final resting place.

Some scenes in the romantic comedy film "The Holiday" were filmed in Godalming - Church Street.

Church of St Peter and St Paul – Godalming

© Tania Kuegler and Martyn Adams

Godalming's Unfamous Residents

BECKHAM JONES

Godalming's least successful Student Counsellor.

By Martyn Adams

Born: March 18th, 1994 in Guildford, Surrey.

Died: ...not just yet.

BIOGRAPHY

Beckham 'Beckers' Jones was living with his girlfriend in a small rented apartment in Tuesley Lane Godalming when he nearly attended Godalming College in September, 2010. He lost his way on his first day. Realising that this was an inauspicious start he decided to write a book of advice (based on his experiences) for other students and co-habiting friends. The book was to be called "The Handbook of Helpful Hints for Guys Like" but was never completed.

An Extract from the "The Handbook of Helpful Hints for Guys"

From the section: *General Tips*

Plastic combs can survive dish washers, even when they're set to 50 degrees C, and they come out looking pretty clean too. (I wonder temperature they melt at?) Manky combs don't do your hair any favours. So when you go home or to your girlfriend's house and you get lumbered with loading the dish washer take advantage and slip your comb in too. Just make sure you unload it before she sees it otherwise you're in deep shit and it's the sort of thing girls don't forget.

There are 4 main types of mustard. American mustard isn't - throw it away. French mustard is the best, it tastes nice and is not too hot. German mustard still has a taste, but is quite hot and only suitable for disguising the horse meat in pork sausages or lasagna.

English mustard is not a food at all. This is a common mistake made by plebes. It is the culinary weapon of choice for all discerning cooks and gardeners. If you see the neighbour's cat poo-ing on your lawn, go outside and make friends with it. Ensure no-one is watching you. Stroke it gently and point it in the direction of your neighbour's window. Put a finger in the jar of English mustard and cover it up to the first joint.

At the right moment stick your mustard covered finger up the cat's arse and release. With a good aim the cat will fly through your neighbour's window and I guarantee you won't be able to stop smiling for quite a while after. It's also great for livening up those dull dinner parties too. For Christ's sake remember to wash your hands after, that's another one of those things girls don't forget.

From the section: *Impressing Mates and Girls*

You do need a cupboard to hold small shot glasses and tall glasses. Get one.

Spirits always taste better from a shot glass. Plastic ones is naff and reusing cups only shows everyone you're a tight-arse. So make sure you have a few shot glasses in a cupboard. They're easy to nick from the local pub.

Wine tastes nicer out of a wineglass, but wineglasses break easy and the glass bits are a real pain when they end up in the sofa or on the carpet; especially if you try a bit of shagging in front of the TV and bits get stuck in her back.

You won't be able to tell if she's screaming in agony or ecstasy. It can be real nasty and the blood stains don't come out of furniture easy either; making it look even more rubbish. Particularly if your parents or the police pay a visit. Furthermore, girls don't tend to forget stuff like that and you end up losing benefits.

Wineglasses are only necessary if you accidentally invite classy girls around to your place, but as classy girls aren't usually shag-friendly, then, unless they're going to bring their own wine - forget it. Wine can be drunk out of the bottle or maybe mugs.

Brandy tastes nicer from a brandy glass but you're a knob if you don't drink it straight from the bottle. If you're trying to impress mates then shot glasses will do. Beer can be drunk from tall glasses too, just like old guys do in pubs, but it's better to look cool and drink it from the bottle or can.

Orange juice and milk tastes nicer out of a tall glass but not if served together. If you're really trying to impress someone then coffee looks really classy if served out of a tall glass. Girls like that, especially with ice and a cocktail hat in it. Don't put veg in a coffee drink though, it ain't Pimms.

If you need to serve coffee but have run out of milk. Pour black coffee into a shot glass and add spirits (e.g. whisky, brandy or that bottle of weird stuff that no-one really likes). This really impresses girls as well as your mates. Recommended.

Before your next party, nick a few of those sachets of ketchup found in cafes. Cut a hole in your girlfriend's favourite soft toy (the smaller ones are best), poke them in and then sew it up again. When you judge the time is right you take out the toy, accuse it of treachery, then stab it (or if it's really small, stamp on it). With enough force the toy will 'bleed' everywhere and you'll come across as being a real cool hard-nut, at least until she realises what you just did. Sadly, she probably won't forget but it's a really great way to break up with her in front of your mates.

Snorting salt to impress – won't. Trust me.

From the section: *Cooking*

Never, ever, ever, fry food while naked.

Never, ever, ever, French a tub of frozen ice cream.

Never, ever, ever, French your girlfriend after eating pickled onions.

Never think erotic thoughts while cooking either. It's more difficult to approach the cooker, and bloody dangerous when it comes to chopping veg.

Wear glasses when removing hot stuff from the oven. Admittedly they do steam up, but they protect your eyes and eyelashes from the sheet of flame when you open the door. Also, if they steam up grey then that's a good sign. If they steam up brown then I suggest you prepare yourself for some emergency culinary surgery (find the scraping knife). But if they steam up black then don't bother proceeding any further. Just close the oven door and phone for your favourite take-away.

Before opening the oven door make sure you're wearing the right gloves too. Those cool 'leather' ones you wear when driving the car are simply not suitable - they take ages to scratch off the door handle afterwards and the remaining bits that are stuck to your fingers (and sometimes the meat) just don't look right – especially if they end up in the salad. Furthermore, if you're serving up pizza, bits of burnt glove are difficult to detect amongst the other bits of burnt topping. Although one can usually improve the flavour with lots of brown sauce.

If you can, keep a saucepan of cold water nearby for those flaming 'eye brow' moments after opening the oven door. If you have guests they will probably find it quite alarming to hear you screaming and/or watching you run to the bathroom with your hair on fire.

From the section: *Recipes*

Fish Fingers on Toast (serves one). Don't make if drunk or hungover. Extract three frozen fish fingers straight from the packet and stack them on their side, one above the other, in one side of the toaster. Toast. When done, extract the three fish fingers and replace as before but in reverse order so that the bottom one is now on top. Add a slice of bread in the other side. Toast again. Extract slice of toast and butter it then, with GREAT care, extract each fish finger (use at least two forks) and place GENTLY onto the buttered toast. If one of those effing fish fingers broke in the toaster - serves you right for not grilling them. Otherwise: Yum!

Don't forget to switch off toaster before poking around with the forks. Electric shocks bloody hurt and for some reason girls don't like white guys with frizzy hair.

Do not use your toaster to reheat pizza slices. Toasters hate pizza. Toasters will melt the cheese off then burn the base. After that malicious act of treachery they'll then need so much cleaning you best just throw the toaster away. However, if you're trying to find an excuse to be dumped by your girlfriend...

For the same reason always add cheese AFTER you've toasted bread.

Despite the heady advance of technology and the incredible usefulness of mobile phones, onions are still very pretty bad news. When cutting raw onions do not sniff them, or better yet, do not sniff at all. In fact, do not cut onions. Replace them in their wrapper and throw them out the window. The 'Intelligent Designer' is asleep on the job and even after a thousand odd years, 'He' has made no progress in making the design of the onion more user friendly.

From the section: *Romance*

If you're at a party and fancy a girl there, then checkout her eyes. If they're droopy then you're in. If they're not, and she's not drinking alcohol then you need to seduce her with a Bunny. A Bunny is a seduction drink invented by an Essex dude who kept rabbits. Take a tall glass, put a shot of fruit juice (black current is good). Add a shot of lime. Add a shot of vodka and top up with lemonade. Put an umbrella in it and she (probably) won't notice the vodka. Get her dancing, she'll drink it quicker. For the second one do the same but use two shots of vodka. For the third one use three – and when she's finished that lot she'll have had six shots and be giggly. Go for it.

If she isn't giggly at that stage then you might as well just give her a bottle of vodka.

Don't keep sachets of mustard in your bedside drawer. Ever.

If it's dark and you're about to shag, then you reach for a condom but instead extract a sachet of mustard but don't realise - and then you tear it open... well let's just say the cold sauce will at first confuse her. Then she'll smell it and probably run outside screaming. Then she'll see it and jump to the wrong conclusion and you'll *never* live it down. Her mates will hate you too.

Explanations never seem to work in these cases.

Ketchup will probably have a similar effect.

From the section: *Living with your partner*

A slice of cheesecake is a real treat if it's served cold from the fridge after a good night shagging. Serve with a giggle at three in the morning. Girls love it and think its romantic.

Packets of crisps might be cheaper but they don't work half as well. Especially if you take them back to bed.

Don't show your girlfriend's dad your collection of flavoured condoms. It doesn't work, no matter how drunk he is or how much you need to bond.

If your girlfriend ever starts talking about god wait for the right moment then point out that he created the universe so he must be an extra-terrestrial alien. Then point out you don't subscribe to UFO cults. If you time it right you'll be able to watch the footie on TV uninterrupted, provided you can ignore her dark looks. Don't expect a shag soon though.

A cup of tea usually tastes nicer if she makes it. If it doesn't, add sugar until it does, but before drinking it ask yourself if she's starting to hate you – and has she added something to the tea?

If you have an argument with your girlfriend before dinner, get a takeaway. Whether she cooks or you cook, either way, you'll lose.

MAGGIE'S LANDLADY

By Christine Butler

'Where am I? What's happening?' I woke up suddenly as someone came into the room. She was carrying a tray which she carefully put down on the floor. 'Who are you?' My eyes wouldn't focus properly and I felt exhausted, not having slept much.

'It's time to get up. Here's your breakfast.' I looked down at the tray. On it was a mug of tea, a bowl of cereal and some buttered toast.

'Thank you. I need the toilet,' I said.

'Ok, I'll take you,' she replied, gently helping me off the hard bed and unlocking the door. I had not noticed her locking it behind her when she came in. 'You don't know what happened last night or where you are, do you?'

'No,' I said, but something was coming back to me. Returning to the cell ten minutes later, for that was where I was, I sat on the bench-like bed and slowly ate my breakfast as memories came flooding back in vivid flashes. In my mind's eye I saw the ambulance and police car arrive. I had called them and I remembered running down the stairs from my rooms to open the door. The ambulance men were not allowed by the police to move the prone figure on the floor of the downstairs bedroom. Then suddenly I was being accused of attacking the old lady.

The terror flooded back and I started shaking. When the WPC entered my cell to collect the breakfast tray she found me in floods of tears.

'Well, you're obviously not ready yet to make a

statement,' she said gruffly, then sat down beside me. 'What's upset you? The memory of what you did? I'm not surprised you're crying.'

'I still can't remember much,' I sobbed, 'just the police coming and taking me away.' Trying to think straight, I managed to ask, 'What am I being accused of?'

'You really don't know, do you?' Her voice had softened. 'Criminal assault. It's a serious offence.'

'I didn't assault anybody. It's all a mistake. I want my father.'

'You won't be allowed to phone him till you've made a written statement. If you're not ready to do that yet, give me his phone number and I'll contact him for you.' Gratefully, I did so and she departed.

Time seemed to drag until she came back with another mug of tea for me. 'I've left a message for him to ring here,' she said. 'When he does we'll ask him to come and collect you. It seems you're to be allowed bail and released into his care. You'll have to come back with him later this week to make your statement.'

I felt as if a great weight had been lifted from me. All I could say in reply was a muttered, 'Thank you.'

While I waited for my father to come I tried to sleep and dozed restlessly. Thoughts rushed through my mind. What had gone wrong in my first term at Guildford University to land me in this predicament? I mulled over the events of the past couple of months, regretting my decision to move out of the cramped little semi-detached house I had been sharing with Sam and Jenny. I wished I had decided to put up with it until I was allocated the promised room in the new Halls of Residence on campus. Surely the work still needed to finish the buildings would be done soon.

As I drifted off into a fitful sleep a vision of the events surrounding my move to my present rooms on the other side of Godalming ran through my mind, like a cine-film. I saw Sam spread the local paper out on the kitchen table after we had eaten our lunch that Saturday. The corners drooped nearly to the floor from the small circle of Formica. Jenny and I were finishing the washing up while she scanned through the advertisements, pencil in hand.

'How about this, Maggie?' she said suddenly, jabbing at the paper with her pencil. 'Two first floor rooms to let in Farncombe. Own kitchen. Use of garden and parking. Let's 'phone now.' She stood up eagerly and reached for the telephone on the worktop nearby, picked up the receiver and dialed the number. 'It's ringing, Maggie. Here you are.' She passed the receiver to me as someone answered.

'Hello, my name's Margaret Johnson and I'm 'phoning about your advert. Are the rooms still available? They are? Oh, they're bedsits. Well, that would do, I suppose. Can I come and see them?' The other two were crowding round me trying to hear both sides of the conversation. 'Where are you exactly?' Mutterings could be heard on the other end of the line. 'Off the Meadrow? I should be able to catch a bus there. How much is the rent? Hm, that's a lot. Still, I'll come and have a look. See you in about half an hour. 'Bye.' I put the receiver down with a flourish, hurriedly found my shoes and coat and opened the front door.

'Hang on a moment, I'm coming with you,' shouted Sam to my retreating back. She hurried down the road after me, leaving Jenny to put away the crockery. As she caught me up she commented rather breathlessly, 'If it's off the Meadrow you'll be able to catch the Guildford bus from there, to get to the university.'

We walked into Godalming and just caught a bus, alighted in Farncombe and eventually found the house in a side road. It looked a bit neglected with faded paint on the front door and window frames, and cracks in the concrete driveway. A ring on the doorbell produced the sound of elderly feet scuffing along the hallway. The door opened to reveal a woman in her late seventies wearing a grey woolen skirt and a thick navy blue cardigan.

'Yes? What do you want?' she looked us up and down as she spoke. Her voice sounded cross and unfriendly.

'Hello. I'm Margaret and this is Samantha. I telephoned you earlier. Sorry it took us longer than I thought to find your house. Can I come in and see the rooms?' This all came out in a rush as the woman's appearance made me feel nervous.

Her face softened as she replied, 'Yes, of course. Come in.' Stepping back, she held the door open. 'Go straight up. There's a kitchen on the first door, with a sink and a cooker.' We followed her instructions and peeped round the door of what used to be the small third bedroom to inspect the barely adequate kitchen.

The next two rooms were locked. She produced Yale keys and unlocked them, revealing a single bed, a chair and a small table in each. 'This room contains a built-in cupboard and there's a wardrobe in the other.' She closed the doors and shuffled along to the bathroom. It looked rather seedy with a stained enamel bath under the window and a wash basin and toilet squeezed in beside it. 'You would have use of the bath in the morning as I use it in the evening.'

I felt depressed as I followed the woman downstairs again. Sam nudged me and sniggered. 'Do you really want to live here?' she whispered in my ear.

'Do you both want a room or is it just Margaret? I

could let you use the two rooms for now, until I get someone else wanting one.'

'That would suit me better,' I replied thoughtfully. 'I think the rent is too high for just one room and a shared kitchen but I'd pay it for the two. How soon could I move in?'

'I'll need references first, and two month's rent in advance. And a breakage deposit.' She paused to let that sink in and added, 'By the way, my name's Mrs Harper.'

We felt subdued as we walked back across the park. I was relieved to have found rooms to rent at last but was not looking forward to asking my father for a loan to pay the deposit. And how long would I have to live there?

Sam spoke first. 'What's the matter, Maggie? You should be feeling over the moon now you'll be moving out to your own place.'

'That's if Dad will lend me the deposit money and write me a reference. I know he's short of funds at the moment.'

'It's giving you freedom and independence,' Sam retorted. 'Be grateful.'

'I am, I suppose.' I said, not totally convinced. 'But I'm still dependent on Dad for my allowance so I'm not really free, am I? My grant doesn't go far'

'You'll have to get a job in a bar or something, to earn a bit of money. I'm thinking of doing that.' We lapsed into silence again until Sam suddenly commented, 'Hey, what did you think of that Mrs Harper? I found her creepy. I don't think I'd like her as my landlady.'

I shivered, thinking about the cold house we had left. 'Don't try to put me off now I've found somewhere to live at last. Still, I know what you mean. I can't put my finger on why she seems creepy. And the way she's arranged things for her tenants seems strange, with the back garden divided lengthways by two parallel paths and clothes lines. I'm not sure whether I like all that pink paint either.'

*****

Hearing a car door slam somewhere I woke up with a start, realising that this slightly strange but apparently defenseless old woman whose house I now shared was the person I was accused of attacking. As I tried to remember what had really happened the cine-film in my head continued to play.

I visualised a car with boxes and bags stacked inside and remembered my move to the flat. We had celebrated afterwards with a very enjoyable meal from a nearby Chinese takeaway. The four of us, including Jeff who owned the car we had used, were sitting around the two small tables in my new sitting room when the door opened and Mrs Harper's face appeared round it. 'I thought so,' she said, 'you're eating Chinese food in my house. I could smell it downstairs.'

'I'm sorry, I didn't know it wasn't allowed', I replied. 'It was cheaper than going out for a meal. I'll open a window.'

'And who's this?' she said, entering the room and looking pointedly at Jeff. 'I don't like male visitors after six o'clock. Didn't I tell you? And I hope your visitors will not be staying late, Margaret. Noise upsets my husband.' With that she left the room, closing the door behind her.

'Oh, my word', gasped Jeff, looking at me. 'Do you really want to live here? Rather you than me.' He took a swig of Coke from the can by his plate. Not long after that we finished eating and the party broke up.

'Would you and Jenny like a lift home, Sam?' Jeff asked. 'Thank you for the meal, Maggie. I hope we didn't upset the old witch too much. Let me know if you need help moving out of here. 'Bye. See you around.'

'Goodbye and thank you again. I'll see you tomorrow at Uni, Sam.' I gave my friends a grateful hug. 'I'm going to miss you and Jenny being around.' The three of them departed and I switched on my small portable television, adjusted the aerial and settled myself on the bed that served as a settee to watch the serial I had been following. Later I made up the bed in the other room and put away some of my clothes before turning in, exhausted but happy.

*****

Someone unlocked the door of my cell, waking me up and driving away the visions just as they seemed to be leading somewhere. 'Bother,' I said, rubbing my eyes as the WPC approached me.

'What's the matter? Don't you want any lunch? By the way, your father eventually phoned us and he should be here soon. I didn't like to wake you earlier, knowing you didn't get much sleep last night.'

'Thank you. I'm beginning to remember things gradually. What did you tell my father?'

'Just that you have been arrested and charged and about the bail conditions. Eat your lunch. You should have time before he arrives.' She left the cell, locking the door. Relieved at her news I suddenly felt hungry and ate the sausages, chips and beans quickly, then sat on the bench trying to remember what had happened.

I thought of Mrs Harper appearing from her living room every time I let myself in to my new flat, but rarely saying much to me. She seemed to be checking that I was alone. Sometimes I heard strange noises in the night such as the sound of doors opening, shuffling footsteps and running water. I assumed that she or her elusive husband slept badly and had to get up in the night. One night a scream woke me suddenly. I was too scared to investigate its origin and had eventually managed to go back to sleep.

*****

An hour or two later my father came to collect me and I was taken to what I assumed was an interview room where he was sitting. A police sergeant was busy completing the paperwork for my bail. Dad looked very worried but smiled when he saw me and greeted me warmly, adding, 'What have you done, darling? Surely there must be some mistake. Have you been formally charged? I gather you have not made a statement yet.'

'Oh, Dad, I'm so pleased to see you. Yes, I was charged last night and no I haven't made a statement. I was too upset to think straight and I can't remember much of what happened yet. It's only just beginning to come back to me.'

'They've agreed that I can take you home as long as I bring you back here in a few days' time. You'll need a solicitor, of course. Now, what do you need from your flat?' He stood up and put his arm around my shoulders as we left the room, giving me a quick hug. I found myself crying tears of relief.

When we arrived at the house we found a policeman standing outside. When I unlocked the front door the WPC appeared and stopped us entering.

'What do you want? You must know that this is a crime scene and that you can't come in.'

'It's also my home and I need to fetch some clothes and things if I'm going to stay with my father for a while. The so-called crime happened downstairs and I live upstairs so I won't interfere with your precious evidence.' I was annoyed at her attitude and my father had to stop me pushing past her.

'But it was you who hit her. Even more reason for you not to go in.'

'Then please let my father in to get my clothes and I'll wait here. You'll need the Yale keys, Dad.' My father shook his head and looked the WPC full in the face.

'If you contact your Police Station you will find that we have been given permission to collect my daughter's possessions from her rooms because she has been ordered to come home with me. Now, please let us in. You can go up with her and watch what she does if you like.'

'That won't be necessary but I don't want both of you up there.' She gave him a disdainful look and opened the front door wider. I disappeared upstairs, leaving him in the hall.

Ten minutes later I came back down, having hastily packed my case and a bag. The WPC came out of Mrs Harper's bedroom, also carrying a bag, and watched us leave.

'She thawed a bit after you went upstairs and she told me she was looking for night clothes for Mrs Harper to take to her in hospital,' my father said, smiling at me. 'She eventually told me that the old lady is still suffering from concussion from her fall and seems very confused, especially about the whereabouts of her husband.'

As we reached Dad's car with my case and bag the boy from opposite called a greeting to me and we crossed the road to speak to him. He was with his father and they wanted to know what had happened. I had chatted with young Jim before, mainly about Mrs Harper.

'I saw the ambulance last night, and a police car,' said Jim's father, eager for news. 'I thought someone had got hurt in the rumpus Saturday night.'

'No, it was Mrs Harper. She had a fall,' I replied,

warily.

'But why the police car? Did they take you in for questioning?' asked Jim, dropping the ball he had been bouncing. His face lit up as he sensed a good story.

'My daughter called the ambulance and the police because Mrs Harper threatened her with a knife,' Dad intervened. 'The police think she attacked her but she says she just pushed her away and the woman fell heavily.'

'Flippin' heck, she's done it again then,' Jim looked worried and glanced up at his father. 'Perhaps this time they'll put her in Broadmoor. Have you heard how she is? Was she badly hurt in the fall? Did you push her hard?' The words came tumbling out as he eagerly questioned me.

My father spoke for me again, 'The WPC said she is suffering from concussion and keeps asking where her husband is. My daughter thought he was living here with her but there's no sign of him.'

The boy's father looked surprised. 'Oh, no, he's been away for ages. When she said that he was in hospital the rumour was that the hospital was Brookwood – you know; the loony bin.'

'Yes, I'd heard that but I thought he must have been allowed home.' I said, remembering what someone had said to me one morning in the local shop.

'No way,' he shook his head. 'Apparently he's suffering from some sort of dementia. Mrs Harper accused him of attacking her so he won't be allowed back here.'

'But was she attacked, I wonder?' My father looked pensive. Something in the other man's demeanour gave the impression that he knew more. 'What really happened then? Can you try to find out? Look, here's my 'phone number.' He handed over a business card. 'Maggie is going to have to stay with me until the court case and she's not allowed to contact anyone here so can you telephone me at work if you come up with anything?'

'Ok, I'll help if I can. As long as I don't have to talk to any police. Come on Jimmy, I thought we were going to the park.' Jim picked up his ball and they departed. Dad and I put my luggage into his car and climbed in. As we drove away Dad commented, 'I wonder what that neighbour of yours knows but is reluctant to tell us.'

*****

The following evening my memory seemed back to normal and I told both my parents about some of the events leading up to that fateful Sunday night, including my first conversation with blond-haired Jim, my young neighbour. He had crossed the road and stopped me one morning as I left my flat.

'You're living in Mrs Harper's rooms, ain't ya? Ooh, spooky! ' He fell into step beside me as I started walking to the bus stop. 'What's she like now? People don't usually stay long. She's weird, that Mrs Harpy.'

'Is she? How do you know?' I glanced down at his cheeky face as he grinned up at me.

'I live opposite, don't I – have done all me life. Me name's Jim. You watch out, miss. I reckon that woman's dangerous. See ya.' He darted off, back up the road, and disappeared.

That evening I told Sam about my encounter with the boy opposite. 'He's trying to wind you up. I'm sure it's just his vivid imagination,' she said, trying to reassure me. But his were not the only comments I heard about my new landlady. People I met in the small corner shop where I bought groceries asked me whether I liked my new home and how long I hoped to stay. One day I asked someone if they had seen Mr Harper recently as my landlady was anxious about noise upsetting him. Her reaction was unexpected.

'He's back, then, is he? That surprises me, after what happened. I thought they wouldn't let him out of Brookwood again. Dear me, we'd all better watch out,' she said, giving me a pitying look as she left the shop. No one would explain her comments, except to enlighten me that Brookwood was a mental hospital, but they all agreed that Mr Harper was mad and it had 'rubbed off on his wife'. After that conversation I made sure that I locked my bedroom door at night.

*****

I also told my parents about a more recent occasion when Jim stopped to chat. Sam was with me. It happened on the Sunday I was arrested. I had spent Saturday catching up on work. After completing my essay I had retired to bed early to read a new novel, eventually falling asleep over it.

Hearing car doors being slammed outside I had woken with a start. Loud voices were topped by a man's drunken shouts and banging on the front door of the house next door. Soon the voices became muffled as their owners entered the house. Then the record player started blaring out pop music. That continued till about three in the morning. I could hear Mrs Harper downstairs, banging on the wall in her attempts to quieten them, and I felt sorry for her. Sleep was impossible for the rest of the night.

When Sam rang the front door bell Sunday morning I was still in bed, having eventually managed to sleep as the sun rose. Mrs Harper let her in and came upstairs with her. She was about to put a Yale key in my bedroom door lock when I opened it, having struggled out of bed and into my dressing gown. There it was, poised ready in her hand. I was annoyed but didn't say anything.

Sam and I had planned to go out for the day but decided to take the picnic she had prepared to Broadwater Lake instead. Jenny found us there later and the three of us wandered back to cook supper in my tiny kitchen. On the way we were joined by the boy from the house opposite.

'Hello. Did you hear the row last night? It must have woke you up. That dope was making more noise than usual and didn't like it when he was shut outside to cool off. We had a good view but you must 'ave 'eard it all.' He looked at me as he spoke and grinned.'

'Hello Jim. That happens a lot, does it?' I asked him.

'Yep, every month. They take it in turns. Mr Harpy hated it and used to run out of his front door yelling at them to shut up and clear off. And one night he got hold of a broom handle and threatened to hit someone but they grabbed it and broke it in 'arf on the front wall so 'e didn't try anything like that again,' the boy added, miming the incident as he spoke.

'No wonder Mrs Harper gets anxious about noise upsetting her husband', I said, thoughtfully. We waved goodbye to Jim and entered the house. Downstairs Mrs Harper was talking in an agitated voice and banging about in her kitchen. 'Hmm, perhaps I won't be staying here long,' I commented as we climbed the stairs to my rooms.

*****

I went back to Godalming Police Station nearly a week later. Dad had found me a solicitor and the three of us travelled to Godalming together. Waiting to be interviewed I was very apprehensive, of course.

My solicitor and I were called into a small room and told to sit down at one side of the table. Two policemen entered the room and sat the other side. After a few formalities one said, 'Now, tell me in your own words exactly what happened last Sunday night.'

The tape recorder was whirring as I explained, 'The noise next door had kept me awake on Saturday night so I went to bed early on Sunday because I was very tired. I went to sleep but was woken up by a loud scream.'

'What noise next door?' said the policeman sitting opposite me.

'It was some sort of party. The neighbours brought friends home with them about midnight. They were drunk and there was a lot of shouting, swearing and banging about. Then they started playing loud music. The noise went on for hours. Some of the banging was Mrs Harper trying to shut them up. She didn't get much sleep and neither did I.'

'What did you do when you heard the scream Sunday night?'

'Got up, grabbed a jumper and ran out onto the landing. When I switched on the light I couldn't see anyone so I crept downstairs quietly.'

'Did you see anyone then?'

'No, not until I pushed open Mrs Harper's bedroom door to check that she was ok and she lunged at me clutching a kitchen knife. I automatically grabbed her wrist and she dropped the knife as she lost her balance and fell sideways. Thinking about it later, she must have hit her head on the edge of the foot-board of her bed – I think she's got an old-fashioned bedstead rather than a divan.'

'Did you look to see whether she was badly hurt?'

'No. I should have done, I know, but I was too scared. I just got out of the room as fast as I could and kicked the door closed behind me. I didn't even look for the knife.'

'And you dialled 999. We have a recording of the call.'

'Yes. I waited upstairs for the ambulance men to come, then went back down to let them in.'

'Thank you, Miss Johnson. That seems clear. Oh, I must also ask you, did you get on well with Mrs Harper?'

'I hardly spoke to her after I had settled in and she had explained her rules. She didn't like my having visitors much because she was worried about noise disturbing her husband.'

'Did you ever see him?'

'No. I could hear her talking to him sometimes and someone gets up in the night to use the downstairs toilet. The plumbing is noisy.'

The police sergeant switched off the tape and spoke quietly to his colleague who had been busily writing during the interview. They passed me the statement he had written for me to read through and sign. While I was doing so my solicitor spoke.

'What has my client been charged with and was she formally cautioned when she was arrested?'

'Yes she was and she is charged with criminal assault.'

'She will be pleading not guilty on the grounds of self-defence.' He stood up to go and I followed his example, returning the signed statement across the table.

'We'll let you know when we want to see you again, when we have completed our enquiries. You may go now.' I thought as I left that there couldn't be much to enquire into, then had the frightening idea that they were waiting in case Mrs Harper died from the fall. A cold shiver ran through me at the prospect of a murder charge. I did not sleep well that night.

*****

Thank goodness I did not have to wait long for my

next interview. On top of the worry, I was frustrated at not being able to attend lectures and see my University friends. Trying to keep up with my studies at my parents' home was not easy. I was very pleased to be told to go back to the Police Station sooner than I expected.

'Well, Miss Johnson, I have to tell you that some interesting information has come to light about your landlady and her husband,' the police sergeant said as soon as we were seated in the interview room.

'What do you mean?' asked my solicitor, looking puzzled.

'I'm about to explain to your client. Miss Johnson, did you know that Mr Harper was in Brookwood Mental Hospital?'

'I had heard that, but I thought he'd been discharged and had come back home.'

'He has left Brookwood but he was discharged to a nursing home because he has dementia. He is not allowed to go back home to his wife. I don't know who she was talking to when you heard voices but it wasn't him.'

'She could have been talking to herself, I suppose. I've never actually heard another voice. Perhaps she's not right in the head, like people say about her husband. Someone told me that he attacked her with a knife.'

'That's what it appeared at the time. Later, finger-print evidence indicated otherwise. So did the old chap's nightmares in Brookwood, according to the case notes. Apparently he told a nurse that his wife had attacked him. When that was followed up none of his prints were found on the knife, only hers. She was not prosecuted because she was considered not fit to plead. Fit enough to be allowed home from Brookwood after treatment, though.'

'So she's done it before,' I said, slowly grasping the

significance of this. My solicitor realised it immediately.

'I assume the knife my client is supposed to have used has been checked for fingerprints?'

'Yes and the results of the check came back a few days ago. That was what threw a new light on the situation. None of the prints matched with Miss Johnson's. Then we received an anonymous telephone call linking this case with the earlier incident between Mr and Mrs Harper. We dug out the old case notes which included a record of Mrs Harper's prints, of course. They matched and no others were found on the knife.'

'So now you believe my client's account of what happened? It was self-defence?'

'Yes, we do. Miss Johnson, you are free to go.'

As we left the Police Station I said, 'Thank you, Jim's father,' quietly to myself.

'Sorry, what was that?' said my solicitor.

'Oh, nothing,' I said, looking forward to returning to my rooms and having the house to myself for the few weeks left of my two months' tenancy. I assumed Mrs Harper would be moving to Brookwood Hospital, this time for good.

Godalming's Unfamous Residents

BRIE GRAM-CNEOW 'THE NAÏVE'

(His true name is unclear, this is a very rough translation)

Godalming's least successful Saxon warrior and supporter of religious reconciliation.

By Martyn Adams

Born: Sometime in the early ninth century

Died: Sometime later in the ninth century

Early Life

We know nothing about Brie's early life (*that's not our fault, it was the dark ages and very little was written around then - okay? And by the way, the 'early ninth century' means from the year 800 to 850 – give or take*). We do know he had nothing to do with a well-known French cheese. In fact we don't really know his name, the name we've assigned him is a rough translation of some blobby (*and poorly illustrated*) texts written on very old monastic manuscripts describing his life (*probably written by a very frightened trainee scribe as an after-hours punishment of some kind*).

As the earliest tales seem to have been recorded some twenty years after his disappearance, we are pretty certain that the details may not be accurate (*but if it's good enough for billion-dollar bible based religions then its good enough for us*).

Later Life

Brie Gram-cneow (*No, we aren't sure how to pronounce it either*) was a young man living in or around the hamlet of *Godelminge* (Pron: Goh-del-minger) or sometimes *Godhelming*. We do not believe this place is where the original 'Mingers' originated. That hamlet was probably much further west in a place known as 'Heerbeallede Mingers' which is one of the very few places in the British Isles where Norsemen invaded, plundered and pillaged - but for some unclear reason never raped. Despite this (or perhaps for the same reason) the population of the village didn't survive more than a couple of generations.

Brie was intrigued by the idea of religion and soon reasoned that the people around him were very impressed by inexplicable natural events such as the weather, the seasons, night time and what the heck was snow anyway? For reasons unclear to him they always attributed these events to the actions of their deities.

In a nearby hamlet called *Tiwesle* (pron: Tiu-wess-leh … *we think. We weren't there so we're really guessing okay? But we get paid 'to know' so take our word for it. It's not as if anyone else is more qualified to argue is it?*) the locals believed in a God called *Tiw* (*so much so they'd named their manor after him. It's now called Tuesley, a quite pleasant name derived from the Saxon for 'Tiw's Clearing' - or the less romantic: 'Tiw's Place Where He Pooed Once And All The Trees Died'*). Tiw (*Also Tyr, son of Odin*) was a God of Law and War. Brie believed this one to be incompetent at managing the weather, which in his mind explained a lot.

However the ruling Danes held to Christianity (*in those days 'Kings' were basically thugs running a regional protection racket. Think 'Royal', think 'Mafia'*). The local Saxons had different deities (*despite what they claimed*). The Celts who passed by held yet other beliefs and yet the pagan Norsemen who came partying through the land (*i.e. pillaging, plundering and raping*) seemed to be having the most fun.

Britain at this time was ostensibly Christian but a lot of the locals only paid lip-service to this confusing religion because, unlike Brie, they had some sense of self preservation. Thus births, deaths and marriages were pretty darned expensive, requiring at least two ceremonies each.

One day, while passing through, a priest described Christianity to Brie but somewhat confusingly – as: (1) a monotheistic religion (i.e. *one God*) but of three parts (*The Father, The Son* and *the Holy Ghost*). This God had a son who: (2) was a liberator - but wasn't a warrior and didn't actually liberate anything; (3) was a king - and yet clearly wasn't; (4) wasn't a God either, but nonetheless should be worshipped as one because he kind-of is. Finally, (5) he could undertake miracles but was nevertheless nailed to a wooden cross and died – but then didn't.

The reason for his death, as explained to Brie, was that 'The Son' had been crucified. He'd cried out to his father for help, didn't get it and subsequently died. But that was good because God, who probably wasn't paying attention before, later resurrected 'The Son' who was now living in an alcohol-free Valhalla somewhere up above the rain clouds (*clearly this didn't sound appealing to either the pagan Norse or the Saxons and caused many to wonder why their brethren, the Danes, had bought into all this. The reason, they figured, must have been financial – it certainly had little to do with logic*). At the same time this son was everywhere else watching everybody all the time while remaining invisible. Furthermore there was also the third element, the 'Holy Spirit' (*neither male nor female, but apparently an 'It'*). This entity was also in Heaven while at the same time everywhere around us and it shouldn't be ignored either - but was anyway.

This confused Brie who knew in his heart that there could only be one single truth. So he decided that what was needed was a grand unified theory of all religions; a natural consensus of opinion to be made by the experts. This would reduce misunderstandings and therefore the fighting amongst the different ethnic groups.

Consequently, and with great optimism, he approached each group in turn and explained his logic. He invited the various religious representatives to participate in his grand unification project. However, each time he did this he got beaten to a bloody pulp. It is from this period he was given the title 'The Naïve' (*or it may have been something like 'The Twit'; sources differ*).

We believe he even encountered a wandering Pict during this period as one tale clearly describes him encountering a naked man painted blue (*or it may have just been a very cold day, we're not sure*). This naked man greeted Brie with the phrase (*roughly translated as*) "What you looking at Jimmeh!?!" And once again, Brie was beaten to a bloody pulp.

At this point Brie had had enough and decided that the only way to convince people of the reasonableness of his arguments was to take up the sword. He reasoned that whoever the real god was, he'd support Brie 'The Warrior of Reason' in his mission to uncover 'The One Real Truth'. Shortly thereafter he encountered a wandering gang of pagan Norsemen (*who were probably looking to 'party' - but in true Viking style*).

From the top of Frith Hill Brie, in a rare moment of unrestrained Saxon savagery, ran down at the gang screaming and waving his sword. Knowing he would be unable to slow down the bemused, and clearly far more experienced, Vikings simply stood to one side and watched him charge past. They then wandered down the hill to find him laying exhausted face down in the dirt. The ensuing struggle was brief but we understand that those pagans did have a party that night.

The following day, now without his sword, his trousers

and with a very sore bottom, Brie decided that a different approach was needed. With self-preservation finally in his thoughts, he decided to create his own religion based upon peace, love and equality. After all, he reasoned, no-one need beat up a man who eschewed all forms of violence.

Brie made his first visit to a monastery, where he knew the monks were quiet, unarmed and charitable. This was quite possibly '*Wokingas Monastery*' (*Woking Monastery; founded circa 690 and losted circa 871 when the 'Christian' Danes - i.e. The Regional Mafia - paid it a 'visit'*). There he was beaten to a bloody pulp for not being a Christian.

The record stops there, but there is a strong hypothesis that Brie, now convinced by the monk's non-verbal arguments and having 'seen the light' (*which was quite probably a near death experience*) converted to Christianity and remained at the monastery. He never quite got to grips with the logic behind his adopted religion and may well have become the very scribe that wrote the original blobby (*and poorly illustrated*) texts.

> **Godalming used to be known as Godhelmin or Godhelminge. But this was well before spelling was standardised, so it also had several other names - as long as they were all pronounced in a similar way.**

THE PEPPERPOT

By Ian Honeysett

It was July 1984 and we had just moved to Godalming from London. The reason we had chosen to live here was two-fold: Petersfield and the Pepperpot. By that I mean, our planned move to Petersfield had fallen through when we lost the buyer for our London flat and, as we drove through towns on the Waterloo-Portsmouth line, we passed the Pepperpot building in Godalming High Street and were rather taken by it. I read that it was called that because it resembled a Georgian pepperpot. It was built in 1814 by public subscription and, over the years, had been used as a court house, administrative centre, a gaol, a market house and a public lavatory.

We were keen to learn more about the town and so, one Saturday afternoon, I left my wife painting the hallway of our new home and joined a guided tour which I had seen advertised in a local shop window.

It started outside The Sun Inn at 2 pm. The guide was advertised as Reginald Trump who described himself as a "leading local historian". As I made my way along Bridge Street, I looked out for a gathering outside the corner pub. It was two minutes to two but all I could see were three people: a small man with prominent teeth and a large hat, a tall thin man with a ponytail and a rather attractive young lady with a rucksack. I introduced myself and the small man welcomed me with rather more spittle than I cared for and said he was, indeed, Reginald Trump. He enquired as to how well we knew Godalming? Sally said she was "passing through" and had never been here before; Mr Ponytail, who otherwise remained anonymous, said he had some knowledge of the place; and I admitted that I had just moved here from London. I mentioned how we had taken to the Pepperpot.

"Well, gentlemen – and lady – you are in for a treat I can tell you. Oh yes. I have been on the radio twice talking about the town. I have also written a book which you may well wish to purchase at the end of the tour. He then collected his payment from each of us, put it in his purse and quickly moved into tour guide mode.

"Godalming is almost certainly a Saxon town. Perhaps dating from the sixth century. It's probably named after Godhelm or 'good helmet' and his 'ing' or meadow. Hence Godhelm-ing!" He looked around with a sense of triumph. It all sounded quite logical.

"It's in the Domesday Book of course." We all nodded. We would have been so disappointed had it not been.

"So let us make our way along the High Street, which has been described as 'tortuously twisting and narrow'".

"By whom?" asked Sally but he had already started to move and crossed to another pub, "The King's Arms".

"We are now outside The Kings Arms which has had many famous visitors including Tsar Peter the Great."

"Not to mention Henry the Eighth," interjected Mr Ponytail. Reginald looked rather annoyed by this. Either it was news to him or it had stolen his thunder.

"Really?" he replied. "A matter of opinion, I should say. But believe it as you wish. Now, shall we proceed? Or would you like to lead this tour?"

We all coughed nervously. Mr Ponytail said nothing. Pleased with his little victory, Reginald continued.

"There are quite a few bars in the town, aren't there?" Sally suddenly queried.

"Bars? Bars?" demanded Reginald in a voice that implied he had been personally insulted. "Not 'bars', madam, but 'inns' or 'public houses'. Please, none of your Americanisms here. This is Godalming, Surrey not… Wichita… er…"

"Kansas?" offered Mr Ponytail. He smiled. Reginald did not. He had clearly decided we were a bunch of trouble-makers. We were beginning to enjoy ourselves.

"In Victorian times," said Reginald, regaining his composure, Godalming had many more public houses than now. In fact, at least 22 – 6 of which were in Bridge Street alone. Not to mention 7 breweries.

"Wow!" exclaimed Sally. "Everyone must have been permanently pi…"

"Inebriated?" interjected Reginald quickly. "That was a problem of course. Personally I never touch the stuff. Give me a nice cup of tea any day."

Somehow we were not at all surprised by this confession.

"I like to get drunk every Thursday," admitted Mr Ponytail. Reginald gave him a withering look but refused to dignify the comment with a response.

"This is The Square, a rather fine building I'm sure you'll agree. Well, most of you at least. It began life as a house, was then given to the borough in 1946 and was used as a restaurant. It now serves as a doctors' surgery."

"I once had a boil lanced there," said Mr Ponytail who was clearly happy to share almost everything with us. "It had turned septic."

"I doubt whether anyone is in the least bit interested in your medical problems," said Reginald sniffily. He looked around for support. Sally and I looked at each other and smiled. She had a particularly attractive smile. I wondered if she were married. Then I recalled that I was.

"It was on my backside," said Mr Ponytail. "It was really painful."

Reginald moved rapidly on towards Crown Court.

"This is Crown Court. It was originally a medieval weavers' court but in 1956 the Council, in its wisdom, decided to demolish part of it in order to create an exit from the new car park. Before long they realised it was unsafe to use the exit into the High Street and so it was closed. By then, of course, the damage had been done."

He looked at Mr Ponytail, waiting for some "smart" comment no doubt. But he simply said that he was sorry but he had to go and so he did. I felt rather disappointed as the tension between the two of them had been the most entertaining aspect of the tour.

We three continued up the High Street. Reginald pointed out where the Old White Hart coaching inn, visited by Drake and Nelson, once stood, which changed use to a builder's yard in 1906. He explained that the first railway station opened in 1845 on the Farncombe side of the river and that, for many years, Godalming had two stations : the "Old" and the "New" and that the latter had gas lighting until the 1960s due to a 100 year contract with the gas company.

We both tittered a little at this. Then Sally said that she also had to leave us as she had to catch a train. She said she was relieved she had a choice of stations, suggesting she had not fully understood Reginald's account. She thanked him for a most interesting afternoon. She gave me a very warm smile I thought.

And so just the two of us came to the most famous building in Godalming : the one my wife and I had fallen for when we first drove through the town. The Pepperpot. And then something very odd happened.

"And so we arrive at what may look like an old, Georgian building but is, in fact, a modern reconstruction."

We looked at each other. Was this a joke? Was he trying to stir up some controversy? I waited for him to explain or laugh but he stayed silent. Eventually I had to break the silence.

"But there is a plaque here on the side of the building which says : "Erected by subscription, 1814, Thomas Haines, Warden".

"Well spotted," replied Reginald with a smile. "All part of the deception. Oh, it's well done I grant you. But those of us, those gallant few, who are in the know, are aware that the original building was badly damaged by fire on November 3rd 1962. The Town Council knew just how important the Pepperpot was to the local economy. It was the very symbol of the town. They called an emergency meeting and ordered the area to be cordoned off, scaffolding erected and draped with covers. If anyone asked, they were simply repairing some of the damaged stonework. But they discovered that the damage was so great that it had to be rebuilt completely. The whole project was completed in just ten weeks. The only sign of their handiwork was a small inscription in the stairwell inside the building, well hidden from passers-by."

"But surely you couldn't keep something like that secret? News would get out, surely?"

"You might think so but the town Council was quite ruthless in ensuring secrecy. It was said that they hired the local Masonic Lodge to enforce it. They had a fearsome reputation. One or two local trouble-makers mysteriously disappeared. One of them, a Mr Hattersley, left town and was never seen again. It was as though nothing had ever happened to the Pepperpot and, to this day, no one mentions the fire and the rebuilding. "

I didn't know what to say. Was it a joke? Reginald Trump looked very serious. If this were his idea of a joke then he was concealing it very well.

Then a thought struck me. If this was all true and it really was the best kept secret in South West Surrey, then why was he now telling me? How did he know I wouldn't tell everyone and expose this breath-taking deception? So I asked him outright.

He looked at me and then began to giggle. "A very good question," he replied eventually. "Do you know, you're the first person to ask me that and I've been leading these tours for many years now. It's just my little joke of course. Well spotted."

I thanked him for the tour and returned home to the smell of fresh paint. A rather odd end to the afternoon but I put it all down to experience. In retrospect I wasn't sure how many of the things we'd been told were true. I never saw Reginald again. I did see Mr Ponytail once in the Post Office and he simply smiled and said "boils".

Several years later, I was helping to put out the Christmas crib at the Pepperpot. It was early morning and the figures of Mary, Joseph and the baby Jesus were kept overnight inside the building. I remember the statue of Mary was particularly heavy. As I was trying to get a firm grip on it, I happened to look down at the side of the staircase. There was some writing there. I dusted it down and could just make out the words : "Lovingly rebuilt by craftsmen of Godalming November 1962."

The Pepperpot was Godalming's town hall until 1908 and was previously known as the Pepper Box

AN INTERVIEW WITH MRS. KATHERINE F. DOLSELEY

Founder Member of the "Godalming Charity for Women In Need of Support"

By Martyn Adams

Scene: Mrs. Dolseley's living room in a large, secluded house in Busbridge, Godalming. The sun is shining through the net curtains and into the room from over the many flower beds in her garden. Present are Mrs. Dolseley (K - age: 93, interviewee) wearing a floral dress and diamond necklace. Barbara James (B - age: 24, interviewer from a local radio company) wearing a black top, close fit jeans and black ankle boots; her assistant / photographer / sound engineer / driver etc. Stephen Johnson (S - age 27) is wearing a suede jacket, white shirt, jeans and hush puppies. Resting on a coffee table between Mrs. Dolseley and Barbara is a large microphone. To one side, staring into a laptop computer and wearing headphones is Stephen.

B: [Into the microphone] This is Bar...

K: Would you like a cup of tea?

B: No. That's very kind of you Mrs Dolseley. This is Barb...

K: Would you like a cup of tea young man?

S: Hm? [Shakes head] No. Thank you, Mrs. Dolseley.

K: I could make you one? Or at least I could get one of my nurses to make you one.

S: No. Very kind, but I'm alright thank you.

B: [Into the microphone] This is...

K: I would have got my butler, O'Neil, to do it you know? But I had to let him go. He was earning more than me, you see.

S: No, that's quite alright Mrs. Dolseley.

K: Can't have that. Expensive. He did that sort of thing though. Make tea, bury the bodies...

B: This is... Bury the… what?

K: Hm?

[Pause]

K: My nurses look after me now. So kind. Not the same as O'Neill of course, but...

B: [Into the microphone] This is Barbara James at the house of Mrs. Dolseley. The date is Thursday the 7th of January, two thousand and sixteen and the time is now nine twenty one. We're sitting in her lounge. We are here to discuss the "Godalming Charity for Women in Need of Support".

K: I know dear. I live here. I haven't lost all my faculties yet.

B: No, Mrs. Dolseley, that's for the record so that we know when and where we made the recording.

K: Why? Don't you know?

B: Yes of course, but we have to record that. For the records, for when we come back to it later.

K: Oh. I see. In my day we used to write on them. Call me Katy. You can call me Katy. But this is a waste of time of you know. Haven't you something better to do?

B: Thank you, Katy. I think this was arranged with you by Paul? My producer? Paul Redgrave?

K: Yes. He was very pushy. Wouldn't let me say no. This really is a waste of time dear. You should go home and do something more productive with your time.

B: Well I'm afraid it's my job Katy. If you don't mind.

K: Well, it's your time I suppose. Are you sure you wouldn't like a cup of tea?

B: No. We're fine thank you.

K: Oh. I would. Stephen dear, that is your name? Would you mind making us a cup tea, would you? I know your mother, you know. [smiles sweetly]

S: Uhmmm. [Glances at Barbara]

K: Please dear?

B: [Nods at Stephen]. It'll be alright. We're recording now, yes?

S: [Nods back, removes headphones and heads hesitantly toward the door]

K: The kitchen's just down the hall dear. You can't miss it. It's the room with the cooker in it. The tea bags are in the tea caddy. I've already boiled the kettle and the tray is laid out ready.

[After another glance at Barbara, Stephen leaves the room]

K: He's a big lad isn't he?

B: [Nods]

K: He reminds me of O'Neil. My butler you know. He was a big man. Oh I do like big men. He made me laugh he did. Big muscles. Lots of stamina. Oh I remember one time... [sighs - pause] Are you two lovers?

B: [Taken aback] Oh, erm. Well...

K: I can tell you see. It's like with my father. He was a

rogue you know. A great man with the women. Flew in the first war. Got wounded in the leg. He always said that he might have a slight limp, but he never was when it mattered. Ha! I didn't know what he meant then. Young and innocent I was. Terence explained it to me after we got married. He was a *rogue* you know. He once told me that I had a large extended family - if I only knew it. Ha! Half-brothers and half-sisters everywhere he said. He was an officer in the Air Force you see? He got posted to lots of places. North Africa, Palestine, Cyprus. He liked Cyprus. Did it hurt?

B: Thank you Mrs. D... pardon?

K: The first time? Did it hurt? You're such a slight thing, I just wondered. Of course he might not be as big everywhere, in which case it doesn't matter does it? One never can tell. Not with my eyesight. It's not the same as it used to be. O'Neil was a big man. All over. I think you can tell by the size of his feet. You don't mind me asking do you? I think he's gentle though. He looks gentle. One can tell you know. Nice man. It's in the eyes. My father always had a twinkle in his eye. [sigh] I do miss O'Neil.

B: Oh. Yes... Katy. I wonder if...

K: My mother knew of course. Well, she would wouldn't she. But she didn't mind. Pragmatic she was. Happy, as long as he came home again. Which he always did. Bless him.

B: Yes... Katy... I wonder if we can talk about the charity.

K: He was loyal that way. Always came home. Not loyal in other ways of course. He was a *rogue* you see.

B: Yes. Katy, might we begin the interview now? The Godalming Charity for Women In Need of Support?

K: I thought we already had dear? Do try to keep up.

B: Oh. I see. No. Sorry. I thought I'd start with a few...

K: My mother wasn't so loyal though. I think she only stayed because of us gels. And the dogs of course. She loved those dogs. But she enjoyed herself too. The cricket team mostly.

\<Pause\>

K: What were you going to ask me dear?

B: Oh, erm. Let's start at the beginning. When were you born?

K: Never ask a lady her age. It's impolite. I was born in nineteen twenty three. On September the Twenty Fifth. I was his Christmas present he always said.

B: ...and you have brothers and sisters?

K: Had dear. Had. I had two sisters and two brothers.

B: What happened to them?

K: Well, Daniel. He died in the war. U boat got him. Torpedoed. Very sad.

B: He was in the Navy?

K: No, no. He wasn't a fool. He was running away to South America. Just unlucky. Then there was Arthur. He flew Hurricanes you know. In the Battle of Britain. He took after his father he did. He died bravely, in action.

B: Ah. You must have been proud.

K: Oh we were. We all were. A fireman killed him when he found him in bed with his daughter. The girls loved the pilots you see. Yes we were proud of him. He bedded most of the girls in North Weald before he died.

B: Oh. When you said 'in action' I thought you meant...

K: What else would you call it dear? Certainly not inaction! Ha! He was *very* active. A very active young man.

Took after father he did. Same eyes, same smile. He was a *rogue* too.

B: ...and your sisters?

K: Yes. There's Elizabeth and Pearl. Betty married a Sicilian and moved out to... Chicago I think it was. Yes. Yes. We lost track of her. Then one day some policewoman came to the house and told us she'd died valiantly fighting the Germans.

B: She fought in the war?

K: No dear. Don't be silly. She was in the mafia. She was known as Bullet-Proof-Betty. Except of course she wasn't. No. The Germans ran a local night club but of course it was in the family territory. So Betty and... Vincenzo... Vincenzo?... Vincy? Was that his name? Yes, that was his name... black hair and swarthy. We named a dog after him. Not such a big man as I could tell. It was a Labrador, I think. Well, they paid them a visit but they were waiting for them. Clever lot the Germans. Then the FBI turned up and arrested them all, well those that were still alive of course. I think I have a newspaper cutting somewhere. I keep it with the forged dollars. Where did I put it?

B: I see. What of your other sister, Pearl?

K: Yes.

<Pause>

B: Pearl? What happened to Pearl?

K: Oh, she's around somewhere I think. We lost touch. Haven't spoken to her in... since... for a long time. Goodness. Goodness, how time flies.

B: I see. How long have you lived in Godalming?

K: All my life dear. All my life. We liked to call ourselves the "O'God Almighties" we did.

B: Who did?

K: We did dear. The "O'God Almighties".

B: Were they your friends?

K: Who?

B: The "O'God Almighties"?

K: Yes. Yes of course. We met at the Women's Institute. The WI. Fine organisation. Where's that tea?

B: This would be, when, the nineteen fifties?

K: Yes. I think so. When did Malcolm die? Yes. That's right. The nineteen fifties. Before they shot Kennedy. He was a nice man. A bit of a rogue.

B: Malcolm. That was your first husband?

K: Malcolm? No. No, no, no. Malcolm was my… erm… Oh dear I've lost count. Which Malcolm was it now...?

B: I thought you had been married twice?

K: Married? Oh, silly me. I thought you said lovers. No dear. I've been married three times. Hm. Yes. The first time...

[Sounds of crockery on a tray at the door, then a gentle knock. Barbara jumps up and opens the door. Stephen enters carrying a pot of tea and tea cups on a tray. He sets it down and pours a cup for everyone.]

K: Oh that's nice. Well done O'Neil. You can tuck me in later. I do like my cup of tea.

[Stephen gives Barbara a puzzled look, then sits back down and puts on the headphones]

K: Where were we?

B: You were going to tell me about your first marriage.

[Katy starts pouring the tea]

K: Oh yes. Well, it was at the start of the war you know. I'd eloped with Stanley – lovely lad. He had a tandem bicycle. He liked bicycles. Big strong legs. He could peddle for the two of us, and he did of course.

B: You ran away and got married?

K: No dear. I ran away with Stanley. I remember we stayed in a small hotel… oh yes, I got oil on my dress. It was a white dress. I was so angry. Well one gets that way when one is young. Or was it floral? That night we stayed in a small hotel. I forget where. It definitely had a lovely lace hem, I remember that. Milford I think. Not far. Separate rooms of course, they didn't allow any hanky panky or anything like that those days; oh no, although the son of the landlord, he was a strapping lad. I forget his name. Anyway, I couldn't see Stanley that night so I spent it with him. Stanley was upset of course. Wouldn't stop wittering on about it all morning. He left later and went home. So I was stuck in Milford with this oil stained dress. I remember, I was so tired that morning.

Anyway, along comes this man. A salesman as I recall. Married of course. Bought me lunch. He booked a room at the hotel. Had his own car. He took me home the following day.

B: Did you stay the night with him?

K: No, no, no. Don't be silly. They wouldn't have allowed that. No hanky panky you see? Although I did of course. Ha! I spent the night with the landlord's son again. What was his name now? I don't think he ever told me. He had a nice smile.

B: So, your first marriage…

K: Oh yes. I got home and started dating Terence. He was a nice boy. Then he got called up, so we got married quickly. Had our honeymoon in Hammersmith. I forget why. He went off to North Africa after that. Royal Engineers. Mine clearing. You know, with those magnet things on poles they swung from side to side. He sent me a photo. Now where did I put it?

B: What happened next?

K: Oh, he dropped it. Bang! Poof! He was blown sixty feet in the air. He always was clumsy. That's why he never got into the RAF. Too clumsy. Funny they should put him in the Engineers. Still, he died flying. He would have enjoyed that.

B: That must have been a sad time for you...

K: No. Not really. Not as I recall. I'd had a nice time in Hammersmith, got a small pension and his bank account. Everyone was nice to me. Then came home. Worked making electric looms for tanks.

B: What about your second marriage?

K: Ah. Yes. Well, that was a completely different kettle of kippers. I fell for him when he was home on leave. He was in the RAF you see. A commander in Coastal Command. He flew those big planes. Noisy things. He was a lovely, big, man. He got stranded in Guildford and we met at a café. I brought him home. He was so nice to me then. Of course after the war things changed. He became an electrician. He used to hold me down you know. Shout at me and punch me. Never in the face, or on the arms. Always the ribs, sometimes the soles of my feet. Bully he was.

B: He physically abused you?

K: Yes dear. I suppose he did. Even the spanking wasn't fun. Thank God for the "O'God Almighties".

B: What do you mean?

K: Well, I was in the WI. Lots of friends then. We made jam, chutney, eider downs, curtains… you know, that sort of thing. It was fun. Painting, coffee mornings... Much more fun than coming home to that miserable old brute. Anyway, I got to telling my friends about him and it turns out that there were several others like me. Some got beaten, some were cheated on. Especially little Ann. Poor little Ann. Her husband would give her a black eye every now and then. Drunken devil he was. She was such a frail little thing too. We all had our problems. So we decided to form the "O'God Almighties". It's a play on words you see. Godalming… "O'God Almighties"…

B: Yes I see. So what did you do?

K: Well we discussed it with Jennifer. She knew about these things you see. She'd studied law and was married to a lawyer. She was qualified too. He worked in the Crown Courts but she was stuck at home with the housework. She hated it. She hated him for making her stay at home all day. Very posh he was though. Always wore a three piece pin striped suit. It looked awful on him. Anyway, divorce wasn't easy in those days. It cost a lot of money and then afterwards you always had that stigma - 'The Wicked Divorcee'. 'The Scarlet Woman'. Absurd! So divorce wasn't really an option, especially if you didn't have any money. And children? Where could one hide? Families wouldn't always help, especially if they were religious. Running away was difficult too – besides, why should we run when we're the ones being beaten or cheated on? You couldn't tell the police, they'd only send you back.

B: Yes. So what happened next?

K: Well we decided to form the "O'God Almighties". It's a play on words you see. Godalming… "O'God Almighties"…

B: Yes, and then...?

K: Well we discussed it among ourselves and decided to do what ever it takes. We only had one course of action really. Jennifer called it "Repudii Simplex". That's Latin. Anyway, I knew a little about electrics, Mary had a little van she'd drive, Paula used to work in a workshop so she knew how to mend it. Little Ann knew a surprising lot about poisons, and Jennifer always helped cleaning up the evidence. She always gave us good advice and did the planning. It's amazing what you can learn in court. You should try it. You can learn a lot. Especially how not to get caught.

B: I don't understand. What did you do exactly?

K: Well, we did our own divorces. Permanent divorce, or widowing as we sometimes called it. Divorces without any of the problems. "Repudii Simplex" you see? Divorce simplified by women, for women. Where the male dominated society, them and all their stupid, bigoted opinions and rules are removed from the issue. So much cleaner.

B: Widowing? You… did you… do you... are you admitting to... Are you saying that you *killed* them?

K: Well, yes I suppose so. Really we wanted to divorce them, but it just wasn't possible in those days. It's what men do. Come up with all those inconsiderate laws. Our husbands would never divorce us, we could never divorce them, so we had to make do. That's what we were taught during the war. To make do. So that's what we did. Ha!

B: You… killed your husbands?

K: Yes dear. Do try to keep up. No choice for us you see? Why do you think the government changed the law to make divorce easier? It's the men, we scared them silly. Bullies they are, underneath it all. When they realised what a group of angry wives could *really* do, well, it's so much nicer now wouldn't you agree? It's easier to divorce than to get married now. Much better.

B: You admit it then. You killed your husbands.

K: Yes dear. Please, please try to keep up.

B: How?

K: Try to concentrate on what I'm saying. Listen to the words, dear.

B: No, no I mean how did you... kill them?

K: Oh, uhm... let me see now. Ann was first. Her husband was a drunkard. Nasty man. Smelly arm pits and bad teeth. One night we waited for him to come out the pub. The Star I think. There was me, Jennifer and Mary. Or was it Paula? Paula I think. She was a naughty one. Ha! I remember once she... But anyway... oh that's right she met him in the pub. She had a bottle of gin, laced with something. I don't know what. She promised to share it with him. She got him completely woozy she did. Then we took him to Queen Street, I think it was Queen Street. We stood him in the middle of the road then Mary ran him down in her little van. Bump! Oh I remember the look on his face afterwards. He looked so confused.

B: He didn't die?

K: Oh yes. Eventually. Mary had to run him over several times. We could hear the bones crunching, between the gears crunching of course. Ha! Then finally Jennifer held his mouth and nose closed. After that we went back to Jennifer's, cleaned ourselves up while Paula cleaned up and fixed Mary's van. Oh we were so, so tired the next day. But it was exciting.

B: Weren't there any witnesses? Didn't the police suspect anything?

K: Witnesses? Possibly. The street lights were out though. I did that. That was easy. If there were any witnesses, well I'm sure they were members of the WI. They didn't rat on us.

B: But the police? Surely...

K: A drunk man run down in the middle of the night? No dear. Happened all the time. They didn't bat an eyelid. Little Ann was confused about it all for a while. God bless her. People kept coming up to her and wishing her the best. She was delighted of course. She didn't know when to laugh or cry. Mind you she cried a lot that one. She even cried when laughing. But she got used to it. In the end.

B: How did you mur..., kill Terence?

K: Oh not until much later. Mary's husband was next. We had to get him out of the way so we could use the van. He was a suspicious man. Mean and nosey too. He gave Mary an allowance of just a few pennies per week and complained if she spent it on a new dress or a new slip. Greasy moustache. Sexy as a breeze block that one. He always complained because she never looked smart. He suspected something was up so we did him the next week.

B: How?

K: Fire. He went to the garage in the afternoon and caught fire. I wasn't involved in that one. I was with Mary, I took her shopping in Guildford, although she couldn't buy anything of course. Came home to find the fire brigade there. It was just as well, I think even Mary would have been upset if she'd heard his screaming. Apparently it wasn't quick, but we were just learning at the time. We were still quite inexperienced. It's not the sort of thing they teach you in school you know?

B: No. No, quite. How many husbands did you... ?

K: "Repudii Simplex"? What's the plural of that? I never did well at Latin.

B: Nor I. How many?

K: Well, let's see... there was me, Ann and Mary of course, Jennifer, Paula – and then later Paula T. and her sister. Margaret Anderson, and Marge B., Dolly, Joyce oh, and what's-her-name... and then there was her, and her sister too. Beatrice, oh mustn't forget big Anne... Anne something or other from Bramley... or was that Angela? Had the big house with the pig sty. That was useful... Then there was woman with lopsided breasts...

[Pause]

...oh I don't know dear, about twenty or so. Maybe thirty, I really can't be sure. It was a long time ago.

B: Thirty? You killed thirty men?

K: Hm. Might have been. There were quite a few. The police got suspicious after a while, a spate of deaths in a small area you see. We had to lay off for a bit. Then some of our members got a little desperate and so we got inventive. Started to make some of them 'disappear' instead. Some of the plans got expensive. We had to hire a coach once and send a couple on holiday. Just so we could bury one in their garden. So we started a little fund, a trust fund. Jennifer set it up for us. That was the start of "The Godalming Charity for Women In Need of Support". Those that could afford it would pay into the fund. Amazingly successful it was. We started running at a profit, then they changed the divorce laws of course. Sad day in a way.

B: So, the charity was initially funded by women wishing to murder their husbands? Seriously? It wasn't setup to help the poor and under privileged?

K: No dear. Godalming? Here? Under privileged? Ha! You might live in a pig sty here but it'll buy you a palace in Wales. Even in those days. Anyway, we never *set out* to murder anyone. It's just that divorce was difficult. Not our fault. We just found a little niche in the market. That's why we called it "Repudii Simplex". We don't do it now. Proves we're not really murderers doesn't it?

B: What about your third husband?

K: Arthur? Oh yes, we did him too. We suicided him. He was embezzling from the post office. That was bad enough but when I found out that he intended to run off with that trollope! Well, …

B: Mrs. Dolseley, you do realise that you've just confessed to murder don't you?

K: Call me Katy dear.

B: Katy... Mrs. Dolseley, you do realise what you've just told me don't you? You do realise what this means?

K: Of course dear, of course. You now have the details of the origins of the charity fund. Clever girl aren't you?

B: But you realise, I shall have to go to the police with this?

K: Ha! No you won't dear. Like I said, it's a waste of time.

B: But you've admitted to murder… to murders. Many murders.

K: Yes dear. And who would you tell?

B: Well, the police. We have the recording.

K: The police? You mean Jennifer's grandson?

B: Jennifer's... ?

K: Hmm. And Ann's. They are both quite high in the force now you know.

B: I could go to Scotland Yard with this.

K: You won't want to do that dear.

B: Why not?

K: Based on the ramblings of a senile old woman? Ha! Besides, the "O'God Almighties" are still going strong dear. That's why. Into their third generation now. They've branched out they have. How do you think we got the divorce laws changed dear? And equal pay for that matter. Wait for the men to do it? Don't be silly. No, no, no. Ha! We had to remove one or two before they got the message, but in the end...

B: You mean... what *do* you mean...?

K: Wives dear. Nobody can apply pressure like a good wife. Why do you think a lot of MPs are gay? They're the psychos we can't prevent getting elected. The others are fine. Usually. They tow the line, under our control. With a bit of persuading. Usually.

B: You...

K: I mean dear, that you'd better leave that recording with me, or you won't sleep tonight.

B: Pardon? I don't...

K: I mean, you *won't sleep* tonight dear. Or your lover boy over there. You'll be dead. *Do* try to keep up.

[Stephen and Barbara trade glances]

K: Like I said. It was a waste of your time. You can't tell anyone. You'll never know if they're an "O'God Almighty" member or not. Or maybe their wife is. We have a lot of contented marriages in Godalming now you know. And we're going to keep it that way. Now hand over the recording.

[Pause]

K: [Turns to Stephen] Hand it over Stephen, or I'll tell your mother. And you don't want that. Do you understand? There's a good boy.

[Zoom in to Katy as she starts smiling at Stephen with

her hand outstretched. Pan around to see Barbara looking at the door terrified. Continue panning to see two women standing there wearing nurses uniforms, dark glasses and dead pan expressions. In their right hands are black onjects, suspicously looking like hand guns with silencers. One nurse has a little teddy bear peeking out of a pocket.]

In 2013 the Waverley area that includes Godalming, was judged to have the highest quality of life in Great Britain and in 2016 to be the most prosperous place in the United Kingdom.

FROGS IN THE CELLAR

By Heather Wright

There were frogs in the cellar at The Grange in Godalming. I really don't like frogs. Well… I don't mind looking at toy frogs or pictures of frogs; they're quite cute… but real ones Ugh! Their slimy green skin and protruding eyes make me shudder and the unpredictable way they leap makes me nervous. I once picked up a frog in a clump of weeds when I was gardening and don't know which one of us was the more surprised but my scream must have been heard a mile away. Perhaps that was when my fear of them started and it wasn't helped by the three men in the house who teased me constantly.

"Don't be silly, they're lovely little things."

"They only jump about to play, they don't mean to frighten you."

"They are more frightened of you than you are of them."

John thought it was great to have frogs in the cellar.

"They will get rid of all the insects," he said.

"That's all very well," I replied," but the freezer is in the cellar and so is the wine and I'm not going down there for anything with those slippery, slimy creatures hopping and croaking about."

"Well you'll just have to ask us to get things for you," he said with a grin as he disappeared into that same cellar knowing that I wouldn't follow.

I lived with it.

Occasionally, when I was desperate for a particular item, I would open the cellar door and listen. Then I would put the light on and creep stealthily and silently down the cold stone steps to the big chest freezer that stood on a plinth at the bottom of the stairs. Then I would open it and scrabble madly for the package I needed after which I would fly back up the steps as if the devil was after me.

I didn't confess to this. I kept it to myself.

So John had monopoly over the cellar. It gave him a feeling of power and he regularly, though gently, mocked my timidity in front of family and friends. Though this resulted in a certain amount of sympathy and quite a lot of mirth, it also introduced lots of froggy presents for birthdays, Christmas and the odd spontaneous gift. I had froggy cards, a froggy nailbrush, toothbrush, pencil sharpener, soap tray and photo frame to name but a few. Ah well, all in the spirit of the game!

Revenge was sweet and entirely unexpected.

One evening I was meeting a friend in a Bistro some distance away. We had booked but hadn't realised that they were having a French Evening until we got there. The atmosphere was wonderful and the restaurant looked great. It was decorated with enormous pictures of famous French buildings, paintings and artefacts and the waitresses wore cheeky black berets, fishnet tights and little short skirts with Basque like tops. The menu was a delight and we looked forward to making our choices, but as I looked around I realised that every shelf, mantelpiece and other available surface was covered in large, lifelike, plastic green frogs.

"Just the place for you," said Bridget with a grin.

I laughed.

"As long as you don't expect me to have frog's legs for

starters," I replied.

An hour or so later, when we were having coffee, I said to one of the waitresses:

"Excuse me, what are you going to do with those plastic frogs after tonight?"

"I don't know," she replied, "they will probably be put away for the next French evening." She paused. "Why, do you want one?"

"I do, yes I would really love one."

She went over to the nearest frog, picked it up and brought it over to me.

"Slip this one into your bag now, we have plenty."

I needed no second bidding. I was glad I had a big bag with me and amused when the frog squeaked as I pushed it in.

All the way home I revelled in my stroke of luck and ran over various plans in my head about using it to my best advantage. When I got home I hid my frog while quite enjoying the vague feeling of guilt as I planned my next move.

The next day I took it into the cellar and put it carefully on the bottom step with its back towards the door. The light was quite dim on the stair but the frog was instantly seen on opening the door. I switched the light off, locked up and went back to mundane chores.

When John came in he got changed and settled with a drink and the paper before dinner. I stuck my head round the door.

"Will you get me a loaf from the freezer please lover."

"Presently," he replied, having been born with a much recognised awkward streak.

"Fine," I said disappearing once more into the kitchen but with a particularly wicked grin on my face. Five minutes or so later I heard him coming down the hall and then the click of the lock as he opened the cellar door.

He switched the light on.

"Bloody hell," I heard, "My God, bloody hell."

"What's the matter. What's wrong"? I said stifling my mirth and trying to sound suitably anxious.

"Nothing for you to worry about darling… no everything's… bloody hell. I've got to show this to someone. What a specimen!"

He came into the kitchen, gave me a distracted smile and went out into the yard.

Everyone knows that John was a "Steptoe" and collected everything collectable, most of which he stored in the yard at the back or in the sheds within that yard. It could have been a beautiful area for eating out or reading a book lazily in the sunshine but had been completely commandeered for what is commonly called junk. He obviously had some particular junk in mind as he went out there muttering with amazement.

About ten minutes after his exit John made an entrance, still distracted and paying me no attention whatsoever. He had a miner's lamp on his head, enormous wellies on his feet, gardening gloves with huge cuffs on his hands and the biggest fishing net you could possibly imagine, under his arm. He strode, like Toad of Toad Hall, through the kitchen and back to the cellar.

He unlocked the door… quietly. He crept into the cellar and you could feel the tension in the air. Would he be able to capture it without doing any damage? Would it escape? Was it even still there?

Silence.

"Oh very funny… very funny indeed," I heard a squeak as he picked up the frog.

"You had me fooled there," he said, "it's very realistic".

He came back into the kitchen removing his gear which he then left on the back step. Saying nothing, he replaced the frog carefully on the bottom stair , locked the cellar door and went back to his drink.

About half an hour went by and Steve came home.

"Fancy a beer?" asked his dad.

"Yeah," replied Steve, "what a good idea."

"Well get us both one from the cellar will you?"

"Not a problem," was the answer as Steve went down the hall and unlocked the cellar door. I heard him shout back to John:

"Hey Dad, where did you get this fantastic plastic frog?"

Humphrey, Jeffrey and Godfrey

THE FURRICIOUS GANG MEET THE WOOF

By Martyn Adams

The Furricious Gang were out for their early morning walk in their home town of Godalming. They are three, rather short, chubby teddy bears called Humphrey, Jeffrey and Godfrey. They live in a secret place near the Godalming Bandstand which is close to a church and to the river.

On this particular morning the sun was shining, the clouds were white and fluffy and the birds were singing – although at least one of them was slightly out of tune and the Avian Musicians Union had been notified accordingly. But anyway, it looked like it was going to be a glorious day. So they decided to walk along the path by the river bank toward the town library.

What is notable about teddy bear walks is that, because they are so short (the teddy bears that is) their walks are quite short too. As you probably know, teddy bears have short legs so domesticated ones nearly always need to be carried everywhere. Wild teddy bears on the other hand go for short walks, usually very early in the morning when no-one is around to spot them.

Godfrey saw something floating in the river.

"Look!" He shouted, pointing to a large, brown thing floating along very slowly and very quietly. "What is that brown thing?"

Jeffrey walked closer to the river, but not too close because he didn't want to fall in. Besides, he was suspicious of brown things floating in rivers. And quite rightly too.

"It's an alligator!" He whispered very, very loudly. "I read about them in a book."

"What's a allin-gator?" Asked Godfrey.

Humphrey, now curious, approached them.

"It's a ferocious animal that lives in rivers." Whispered Jeffrey, managing to make his whispering much louder than if he'd just spoken normally. "They have little eyes, big teeth and they bite."

"Do they eat teddy bears?" Godfrey asked, tears welling up in his eyes.

"Oh yes. Teddy bears is their favourite food."

Just then the alligator thing must have bumped on something. It shuddered, sending ripples across the surface. Then it turned as if to look at them.

"It's seen us. Run!" Shouted Jeffrey, and he started running away - past Godfrey, past Humphrey and back down the path towards home. His little legs were just a blur of motion. For a little bear he could run amazingly fast.

Humphrey was about to turn and run too but stopped because Godfrey was still standing, frozen in fear like a bunny rabbit caught in a car's headlights. The silent menace came to a halt against the river bank, bumping it's nose against a small tree stump causing even more little ripples of water to flee from it in all directions.

"But I don't want to be eatened!" Whimpered Godfrey.

"Then run you daft ball of fluff!"

Humphrey grabbed Godfrey by his left ear and the two started running away.

"Are allin-gators - fast?" Panted Godfrey.

"That doesn't - matter as - long as you - stay right - behind me." Shouted Humphrey, his legs whizzing back and forth.

"Can allin-gators - climb trees?"

"What? Brilliant! Here, stand by this tree." Humphrey skidded to a stop by a tree and grabbed Godfrey before he could run past.

"Why?"

"Because I don't want to be eaten. Here, hold my foot."

Godfrey bent down and grabbed Humphrey's raised foot. Humphrey proceeded to climb up Godfrey as if he was a ladder, first stepping onto his shoulder then his head.

"Ow. Ow. Ow!"

Clasping the trunk of the tree he managed to climb up and held on to the trunk.

"Grab my feet!" He yelled and Godfrey jumped up and grabbed one of Humphrey's feet. With a lot of huffing and puffing and with immense effort both of the bears finally managed to pull themselves up onto a branch.

They looked down.

"I don't see the allin-gator."

Humphrey thought a moment longer. "Bloody thing is probably sneaking up on us. Let's climb further up."

And so the two bears climbed up the branches until they were hidden deep inside the canopy.

They both looked down. It was clear they were not being followed.

"Phew! We've lost him."

"Phew!" Said Godfrey.

"Hullo." Said a deep gruff voice.

Godfrey squeaked like a mouse and nearly fell off the branch. Both of them slowly turned, eyes wide with fear, to look upon a small dark furry dog-like animal with big brown eyes and a very bushy tail peering back at them.

"You're not an allin-gator." Declared Godfrey. "You've got big eyes and you're not wet."

"Oh good. That's nice to know." The animal smiled back at them, in a friendly sort of way. "Would you like a cup of tea?" He asked.

"If you're not an alligator, then what are you?" Whispered Humphrey.

"...and do you eat teddy bears?" Squeaked Godfrey.

"I am a Tree Woof." Said the Tree Woof. "I only eat beetfruit, and this is my tree."

"Oh. I'm so sorry but I..." Humphrey relaxed a little. "We were chased up into this tree by an alligator you see."

"Oh. Really? I didn't know there *were* any wild alligators in Surrey. I thought they liked to live in zoos. Would you like a cup of tea?"

"Do you have any biscuits?" Asked Godfrey.

"...sorry about the mess on the branch." Whispered Humphrey, his cheeks reddening.

"That's alright." Said the Woof. "I'm sure it'll deter the Scribbles."

And so the two bears gratefully accepted the Woof's

offer and followed him into his secret little home inside the tree. It was very cramped with the three of them, but very cosy. It had little chairs, a little table and a window with real glass.

"I've never met a tree woof before." Declared Humphrey. "What should we call you?"

"You can call me Woof. As there are so few of us around, we don't really bother with names."

"Oh." Sighed Humphrey. "That must make school registers pretty confusing. Tell me, are you a boy or girl Woof?"

"Boy." He smiled "Can't you tell?" With a slight glint in his eye.

"Probably." Said Humphrey diplomatically keeping his eyes straight and level. "Are there many like you hereabouts?"

"No. There are not many of us about. Particularly here in Godalming. We are an enstrangered species. That is, we're not endangered, just very strange and very secret. Few people know about us. Like the Beetfruit trees. I think this is the only Beetfruit tree for miles and miles."

Humphrey frowned. "I thought this was a weeping willow."

"Beetfruit trees disguise themselves because their fruit is so nice to eat. Only tree woofs and scribbles know how to find beetfruit trees. Do you want to try a beetfruit jam sandwich?"

"Yes please. Yes please." Said Godfrey who started bouncing up and down in excitement, rocking the tree slightly.

"What's are Scribbles?" Asked Humphrey.

"Pests, basically. They look very much like small grey

squirrels, but they are spotty, grey and black, and their tails are not so wonderfully bushy as a squirrel. Nasty, untidy things. Always losing their nuts and fighting amongst themselves."

So the two bears had a beetfruit jam sandwich which, they soon discovered, was very tasty.

"That was very nice." Said Humphrey. "Rather like raspberries but with strong orangey tang. Tell me, do they distil?"

"Distil? I don't know what you mean."

"You know, like juniper berries into gin? Grapes into wine? Or maybe rye into... ?"

Humphrey looked into the woof's eye's for any sign of recognition. But there was nothing there.

"I really don't know."

Humphrey smiled and his ears stiffened. He sensed a new business opportunity.

"Perhaps we could acquire some beetfruit from you?"

"Certainly, I have plenty. I'm sure we could find something to trade."

Godfrey perked up. "Why are you called Tree Woofs?"

"Oh that's because we look like a little dogs and we can bark like dogs so people mistake us for dogs. We often pretend we're dogs so that humans don't recognise us. We're not of course, because we live in trees."

"Are there any other kinds of Woofs?"

"Oh yes. There are Bush Woofs. They are smaller than us and live in Australia, but I don't know if they live in bushes or in The Bush. There are Jungle Woofs too, but they are so secret few know about them. Then there are the most secret and furricious of all the woofs – Roof

Woofs."

"...they live in roofs?"

"How did you know that?" Demanded the Woof, shocked that Humphrey already knew of their secret.

"Just a hunch." Shrugged Humphrey. "Well, thank you for the tea and the biscuits and especially the beetfruit. We had better get going." He said after a while. "Soon people will be about and we would rather remain secret. Wild teddy bears like us would like to stay an enstrangered species too."

"I perfectly understand." Said the Woof.

"And don't forget about the beetfruit. I'll be in touch."

So the two bears left the Woof's little house and scrambled down the tree, making sure there were no alligators on the footpath first. Then they ran as fast as their little legs could carry them back to their own secret hideout, where they found Jeffrey waiting for them. He was very worried.

"Where have you been?" He asked. "I got so worried I ate all the chocolate biscuits."

"Of *course* you did." Sighed Humphrey, rather grumpily.

Godfrey explained how they hid in the weeping willow only to discover that it was really a Beetfruit Tree in disguise, and also home to the only Tree Woof for miles.

"I heard about a rough Roof Woof once. He was just riff-raff though." Said Jeffrey.

Humphrey gave him a most peculiar look. "You *are* referring to a *rumoured* rare rough riff-raff Roof Woof...?"

"Well... yes. I suppose. He was wearing..."

"Don't you *dare* say Elizabethan neckwear!"

Jeffrey fell silent, puzzled by Humphrey's exasperation, but knew better than to continue.

"Now then, my little gang of furricious furry friends, we have a problem. We need to defeat the alligator and, at the same time, find something we can trade with the Woof, while at the same time being able to carry it all back and forth between our secret hidey hole and the Woof's without being noticed. And we need some tanks and some pipes. Lots of pipes. Copper ones preferred. Ideas?"

"We could build a tunnel." Said Jeffrey.

"It's a pretty long way from here to the Beetfruit Tree."

"Maybe we could build it to the river, then build a boat?"

"Hm. It doesn't bother you that our secret hidey hole here is below the river level?"

Jeffrey looked puzzled, So Humphrey explained the issue slowly.

"So we build a tunnel, under the riverside path and up to the river."

Jeffrey nodded.

"A single, amazingly pipe-like, tunnel leading from our nice dry dining room straight to the side of the very, very watery, water filled river?"

Jeffrey's face was blank, reflecting closely his thinking.

"Do you follow me?"

Jeffrey shook his head.

"The water would pour in and flood our home?" Suggested Godfrey – who was ignored.

"What's to prevent an alligator from deciding that our tunnel looks just like a handy underwater pipe leading to a

Teddy Bear snack bar?"

Jeffrey thought for a moment. "We could put a door at the end of it?"

"...and the alligator wouldn't be curious to know what's behind the door?"

"A one way door?" He ventured. "With electronic locks? And an underwater camera?"

"Fluff for brains! You're just a ball of fluffy fluff aren't you? Good grief! If God needed intelligent fluff, well, he'd know to sweep it up from under his settee - because that sort of fluff is far more intelligent than your little pathetic excuse for a brain. Look, if we built a tunnel to the river everything that swims by would see it and want to pay us a visit. Like a shark for instance, or the wild Lesser-Spotted Bear-Eating Garden-Variety Hammerhead Octopus."

"Uh." Nodded Jeffrey, seeing Humphrey's reasoning.

"What about the flooding?" Asked Godfrey.

Humphrey ignored him again. "Besides, I know for a fact that launching a rowing boat underwater doesn't always work."

"Why not?"

"Wouldn't the river rush in and make our biscuits wet?" Suggested Godfrey in vain.

"Because the rowers get very, very soggy even before they start rowing, and the boat just goes more downwards. In fact rowing with oars on the bottom of a river just digs it in more. That's why ancient Nordic Teddy Bear cruise ships, what the humans think are Viking Long Boats, are all buried in river beds or at the bottom of Fjords. The bears kept rowing even when they'd been sunk - probably by the Vikings. No. I'm thinking more along the lines of a camouflaged transport, like a cart."

"I like cars." Offered Godfrey.

"I said cart. Although putting an engine in one sounds like a pretty cool idea."

"We could drive it along the path, to the Beetfruit Tree." Said Jeffrey.

"Precisely!" Said Humphrey.

"And we could drive it back."

"Give the bear a banana!"

"I like bna-bnas." Said Godfrey.

"Bananas." Clarified Humphrey.

"Bna-bnas." Offered Godfrey.

"What if the alligator leaps out and bites us?"

"It'll have to be an armoured car." Said Humphrey.

So that night and the following day they set about building an armoured car. The following morning was a disappointment though. They'd built the armoured car from bits of corrugated metal they'd collected as scrap over the years and lots and lots of bits of string. The engine was an electric motor from an old washing machine, and an old car battery was to power it. The wheels were taken from discarded (or sometimes 'borrowed') push chairs.

What they'd forgotten was how to get it out.

So for the next three nights they improved the armoured car by putting a little turret on top for Godfrey. It was made from an old metal bin lid which sat on his head tied by a chin strap. Provided he didn't turn too quickly he could see in any direction. However if he *did* turn too quickly then he'd spin around and around and end up facing the wrong way.

They also added cushions because inside the car there were bits that were hard and pointy. Teddy Bears do not like hard and pointy things, so that meant using a lot more sellotape and string to tie the cushions to the right places.

Most of the bear's work was digging a ramp for the vehicle to come out near the riverside path. The spoil was dumped into the river which washed it downstream. Some was scattered over the lawns, but definitely not the Godalming Bowling Green – that was holy ground to the bears. They often watched the Godalming and Farncombe Bowling Club through their secret periscope. It is one of the many perks of living there. And besides, Humphrey ran a betting syndicate. So far he had acquired a tidy little pot of coins, buttons and biscuits. Especially biscuits.

When that was all done they decided to take the car for a test drive.

It was very early in the morning when they wheeled the armoured car out onto the path. The sun was barely above the horizon and the birds were singing – although one of them was still out of tune and the Avian Musicians Union had been notified again. But this time with stronger wording.

The bears climbed inside the metal contraption and tried to start the engine. It didn't start.

"Rats!" Exclaimed Humphrey.

"Where?" Asked Jeffrey peering out a peep hole.

"I don't like rats!" Squeaked Godfrey, spinning around and around in his little turret, frantically trying to spot them.

"No. I mean: Curses! The engine doesn't work."

"Oh." Said Jeffrey, as helpfully as he could. "Perhaps the battery needs more petrol?"

"Batteries don't use petrol." Said Humphrey. "Hang on... what do you mean *more*?"

"Uhm..." Said Jeffrey, as helpfully as he could.

"Okay. Plan PP then." Sighed Humphrey.

"What's Plan PP?" They two bears chorused.

"Pedal Power. We use the pedals." Humphrey looked around for the pedals. "Where's the pedals Jeffrey?"

"Uhm..." Said Jeffrey, as helpfully as he could.

"You forgot to add the pedals didn't you?"

Jeffrey only nodded. He'd run out of helpful 'Uhms'.

"In that case its Plan PPP."

"What's Plan PPP?" The two bears chorused.

"Paw Pushing Power! Jeffrey and I shall grasp the sides of the car and we push with our feet. Let's see how fast we can make this thing go."

It went surprisingly fast, at about teddy bear walking speed (about a metre per second) or half-human walking speed. That is, one would think it would go very, very slowly but you must remember that teddy bears have really short but thick legs and so they have quite a good push-to-weight ratio. It's this same ratio that enables them to climb trees, or steep stairs.

Teddy Bear space scientists once built a special apparatus that enabled ten bears to push planks of wood. Each bear's plank had another bear pushing a plank on top of it. So the topmost bear was propelled forward by the nine bears below him. An eleventh bear, called an 'astrobear' wearing a helmet and goggles, was sitting on the top plank. He was accelerated forward at ten metres per second per second, or one G. Of course he fell off well before he could accelerate into orbit. That's just one reason why the Teddy Bear Paw Powered Space Program didn't take off. The astrobears didn't.

"Return to base. We'll have to do without the engine."

Godfrey spun around to face the back.

"Argh!" He wailed. "The steering wheel's fallen off."

"Daft bear! We'll have to add another one for going backwards. Turn around Jeffrey."

"How?"

"Not you Godfrey. Jeffrey. Turn around... Right off we go backwards."

It took a lot huffing and puffing, end even lifting the armoured car a few times, but eventually they got it back into its secret underground garage. They closed the grass covered roof and set about improving the car. This entailed removing the petrol filled battery and the engine and then adding a second steering wheel so that Godfrey could steer when going backwards.

That night the bears were very, very tired and they all slept soundly.

The next morning they tried again. This time plan PPP was put into action from the start. They got half way along the river side path before Humphrey and Jeffrey fell down inside absolutely exhausted. Fortunately Godfrey had remembered to bring some refreshments including: -

Six packets of newly purchased chocolate biscuits

Six jam sandwiches

Three marmalade sandwiches

Three cheese sandwiches

A bottle of pickled onions

A jar of pickle, loaf of bread, tub of butter

Three cups and saucers

A teapot and a kettle

A gas burner with a spare gas cylinder

Assorted cutlery and crockery

A small sausage cooker

Small vegetarian party sausages

Party hats, poppers and those blowy, wheezy, squeaky things

A balloon (with a hole in it)

A battery powered refrigerator with batteries

Extra blankets and cushions

A rubbish bin with extra liners

An emergency get-away tricycle (Godfrey sized)

You get the picture...

This lot almost certainly accounted for the extra weight of the vehicle but teddy bears don't think that way. To a teddy bear a picnic is an essential part of any enterprise, which is one reason why teddy bears never conquered the world – at least, not in the military sense. In fact, teddy bears never really grasped the human concept of warfare – not when their opponents might have an interesting new snack to offer.

It's also another reason why the Teddy Bear Paw Powered Space Program wasn't successful. It's very difficult to dunk biscuits, let alone pour tea, in zero gravity.

It's also the main reason why the Teddy Bear Bungee Powered Space Program didn't work either. Early experiments showed that pickled onions bounce around inside space helmets and interfere with an astrobear's hearing. Some even slide down their backs tickling them to exhaustion. NASA have many secret recordings of giggling space bears they have yet to decipher.

"We have - to think - of an - other way." Puffed Humphrey. "This is - too much - like hard - work."

Jeffrey was speechless. He fell over backwards and Humphrey had to revive him with an orange juice and cheesecake.

"What we need is a service station." He thought. "Just about here."

Godfrey had got bored and was already asleep, chin still strapped into the bin lid, when Humphrey and Jeffrey decided to take a nap. So when there was a gentle scratching on the side of the car it was Godfrey who woke up first. He sat up, poked his head out, turned slowly and looked down to see Snowy the Pole Cat.

"Hello Snowy!"

"I thought it might be you. Hello Godfrey. Why are you parked here?"

"We've just had a picnic and Humphrey and Jeffrey are still asleep and we have milk and cream and spoons and cookies. Would you like some?"

So it was a complete shock to Humphrey to wake up with Snowy sitting on his head, enjoying a plate of cream.

"Emufe me! Mut your mig murry mum in on my mafe!" Muffumbled Humphrey as he poked at the cat's posterior.

Snowy reluctantly rose and found a cushion to sit on.

"Thank you."

"Did you say I had a big bum?" She asked politely, but with the sort of pointed politeness that also threatened a slow, screamingly painful death should the answer be unsatisfactory.

"No...?" Answered Humphrey in all innocence. "You must have mif-heard."

The furricious gang then discussed the problem at hand. Humphrey was adamant they needed to find a way to transport beetfruit for his new distillery. Jeffrey was adamant the armoured car needed more wheels because the more wheels you had, the faster you went (which is why, he reasoned, that roller skates had so many wheels). Godfrey was adamant that on the next trip they should have a separate fridge for the cream buns.

Snowy was just exasperated. In the end she solved the problem for them.

"Why don't you ask the Woof to deliver?"

The bears fell silent, eyes wide, mouths open, shocked with the simple elegance of the solution. Still open-mouthed they watched as Snowy elegantly left the vehicle, then elegantly leaped to the ground. Then, as cats do so well, she elegantly strode toward the bird song that was clearly still out of tune. It was time for a savoury breakfast - sponsored by the Avian Musicians Union.

So if you happen to be walking along the path by the river in Godalming very early one day, and you spot what looks like a small black dog, with a bushy tail, big eyes and carrying a bag of something in its mouth. You'll know that it's not a dog at all, it's a very rare and enstrangered Tree Woof delivering beetfruit to a secret location near the Godalming Bandstand.

And should you see what looks like a pile of corrugated iron on wheels, sneak up to it, put your ear against the side and listen. If you're very quiet you might hear the bears inside having an early morning picnic breakfast in their new Armoured Picnic Car. Moreover, if they're singing, hiccupping and slurring their words, you'll also know that

Humphrey got the beetfruit distillery working.

But even if you don't see these little Godalming treasures, you might like to note that there's at least one fewer bird in the dawn chorus; but those that remain are *always* in tune.

JJ Burnel, bass player of The Stranglers, grew up in Godalming.

THE HONEY CAKE

By Heather Wright

It started when Virginia Gordon bought her husband a goat for his birthday.

"He wasn't a bit pleased," she told me in amazement, "but he always seems to be out mowing the grass at the weekend and I thought this may be one way we could see more of him".

She seemed offended by his lack of gratitude.

"I wouldn't be a bit pleased either." John said when I told him about it.

"But what an unusual gift." I replied, "I love to be able to find things that are a bit different for presents."

John looked worried.

"Well, don't even think of buying a goat for me." he said firmly.

*****

A few months later, when staying on a farm in Devon, we were very impressed by the home produced honey served with breakfast and went out with the farmer later to see the hives.

"I wouldn't mind keeping bees myself one of these days," John said thoughtfully.

I didn't reply but was processing the information with interest. He had a birthday coming up in a couple of months and his idle comment seemed to me to be a nudge in the right direction.

170

I consulted with the boys.

"Good idea," said Steve. "Are you going to get the hive then?"

"I thought I might."

"Great, then I'll get the hat with the veil thing… you know."

"Martin?" I looked at him questioningly.

"Yes, well I'll get some of the long gloves…what did the farmer call them… gauntlets?"

The whole scenario really appealed to me but needed a bit of research. I looked for adverts in the gardening magazines and eventually found one offering hives at what I thought was a reasonable price. New and empty of course.

"I'll need to get him a Beekeepers suit too," I said to my partners in crime, "they're like white overalls."

"Yes, and a book that tells him what to do with it all."

"Crikey," I muttered. "I'll need a bank loan by the time I'm finished."

Gradually we got the gear together and managed to keep it well hidden prior to John's birthday. Then on the eve of October 21st we assembled everything into a sort of display in the conservatory and closed the curtains. It was all very clandestine and we felt rather pleased with ourselves I think I even rubbed my hands together with glee. I was dying to see his reaction.

He dashed off at the crack of dawn the next morning so the curtains weren't opened until he got home that evening, had changed out of his suit and had a gin and tonic in his hand.

"Sit down," I said.

"Why?" he replied, being John.

"You'll see." At that point the boys drew back the curtains to reveal the brand new hive surrounded by the various relevant items an apiarist might need.

John gawped. There is no other word for it. He was staggered.

"Well Dad," said Martin, "what about that then?"

"I don't know what to say."

"Well, what about Buzz buzz?"

"Very funny."

He looked at everything in turn, each having a gift tag with a message from the donor.

"Well where do I get the bees from?"

I knew. I had checked that out and was able to tell him a number he could ring to be advised about getting a swarm.

"You'll have to read up on how to knock the swarm into a box. Then you have to put a white cloth over the slide into the hive and the bees will walk up it into their new home."

John grinned at me.

"You've got it all sussed out so perhaps you had better do it."

"No chance mate. You are the apiarist from this moment."

*****

As you might imagine, the process of finding a swarm and then transferring it caused lots of tension but even more laughs. Suffice to say at this point that all went well and John's enthusiasm confirmed for me that I hadn't made the same mistake as Virginia.

Of course, being John, he went out and spent a fortune on other accessories like a smoker, a honey separator and so on, not to mention getting labels for Catteshall Honey printed before there was even any sign of honeycomb!

There was one day, the following summer when I was sunbathing in a bikini with a friend when John came out of the house all dressed up in his bee keeping gear. He had on his white suit, gauntlets, hat, veil and Wellington boots. He was going to smoke the bees to make them drowsy then intended to divide the swarm having, in his enthusiasm, bought another hive by then.

"You'd better get some clothes on if you're coming to watch." he said.

"We'll be fine," I replied.

"Be it on your own heads then when you get stun,." said the pompous beekeeper setting his smoker going.

The bees buzzed and flew about angrily, gradually quietening as the smoker became effective. It is interesting to record at this point that the carefully protected beekeeper got thirteen stings that day and the bikini clad spectators got none!

*****

So the bright idea became an all absorbing hobby and eventually John joined Beekeeping societies, bought books and more equipment to support his venture and quite soon began to process some honey. The prematurely purchased labels were soon in use and boxes of honey jars were ordered on which to stick them. I won't go into the details of sieving the honey to acceptable guidelines and transferring into the jars. Suffice to say that it was a sticky business. No-one grumbled though when they came to eat the produce as it was absolutely delicious.

PART 11

"They've sent the tickets for the honey show at Earl's Court" said John one day the next summer, "They've also sent details of the programme which means that I must be getting the honey ready for showing fairly soon."

"Mm, Mm." I replied with my mouth full of toast.

"Hey… guess what… there's a competition for the best honey cake."

"Great." I muttered with little enthusiasm.

"You'll make one won't you?"

"Me?"

"Yes. Go on that would be really good."

"But I don't do cakes."

"You can though… go on, they give you the recipe to use."

"Well what's the point of everyone making the same cake?"

John sighed with frustration.

"It's a competition for God's sake."

I carried on munching my toast while struggling to concentrate on the cryptic crossword.

"Well anyway… no… I won't."

John stumped out muttering something about unsupportive wives and looking very grumpy.

Later on that day I took a look at the recipe and decided to give it a whirl. Was it guilt or was it challenge? I still don't know.

I have to confess that I am not good with recipes as I would rather make things up as I go, so, in addition to the ingredients written on the sheet headed "Honey Cake" I threw in a few extra touches of this and that: a tablespoonful of orange juice, a pinch of nutmeg and so on.

The cake looked OK when it came out of the oven and I put it on a rack to cool.

"You've made one," said John following his nose into the kitchen, "It smells marvellous. You're a star."

I must admit I was feeling rather pleased with myself and responded warmly to his hug and kiss.

On the day of the show I put the cake into a tin with a doyley and a pretty plate, John piled the car with jars of honey for the various categories in the showing section and off we went.

Pushing through the surprising melee of Honey Show enthusiasts we shed the jars at the appropriate tables eventually coming to the stand showing the entries to the Honey Cake Competition. My eyes nearly popped out of my head when I saw it.

"Oh… my… God," I said.

I couldn't believe it.

Every cake was presented in an extremely elaborate fashion with decorated stands and intricate flower arrangements. One was displayed between gold sprayed twigs on a silver cloth, another on a plinth with a china figurine leaning towards it and there were drapes and baskets of fruit everywhere. Each cake had a name and category label printed both artistically and professionally in beautiful Italic script.

I had a cake, a plate and a doyley.

"That's it," I said, "I'm not putting it in."

"You are."

"I'm not. I AM NOT PUTTING IT IN."

"Well I will," said John writing John Wright on the plain piece of white card I had brought.

I went and left him to it. Wandering round the stalls and displays, I bought some hand cream and body lotion (honey based of course) and went and had a coffee. I could hear the results being called over the loud speaker and see the crowds rushing over to each category as it was called. The air was dizzy with the warm smell of honey and the excitement and enthusiasm was almost tangible.

Then I could hardly believe what I was hearing.

"And now the judges are ready to name the winner of the Honey Cake Competition. The first prize and highly commended goes to Mr John Wright of Godalming."

They went on to say who had won second and third places but I was too busy making my way over to the appropriate stand to listen.

All the cakes had been cut into bite sized pieces for the judging. The silver cloth that covered the table was littered with currants and crumbs and the gold twigs and various ornamental decorations lay here and there amongst the debris. Floral displays had been knocked over and the fruit had rolled inelegantly out of the arrangements. In the centre was my plate surrounded by people having a taste of the winning cake. John stood there, red certificate in his hand looking proud.

"What did you put in your cake to give it this 'je ne sais quoi'?" I heard someone ask.

"Oh, this and that… you know," he replied. "Oh, here's my wife. Come over here darling." I could hear the relief in his voice.

"Mrs Wright, how proud you must be of your husband," said one of the judges.

"Yes."

"Does he bake regularly?" asked another.

"You could just call it a one off," I replied with a sweet smile taking the last bite sized piece of my own cake.

PART 111

So beekeeping and processing the produce gave John a lot more joy than if I had bought him a goat. Over the last few years he built up to five hives, all facing up river and well down the bottom of the garden amongst the heather. We had no casualties with stings and always had a pot of honey to take with us wherever we went. When he died, the crop had been harvested and there were 98 jars of Catteshall Honey in the cupboard.

They say that you should always tell the bees when there has been a death in the family and it was as if they knew. They were certainly very unhappy and a few people commented on seeing a lot of bees around at the funeral.

The honey in the cupboard lasted for about ten years… but the memories linger on.

LESS FAMOUS POTTER

By James Tong

Hi my name is Larry Potter. Many of you may have heard of my more famous older brother. However any likeness to any person or persons, or any adventure real, fictional, or otherwise is purely coincidental, as I have not been involved in, and nor have I had anything to do with my more famous sibling.

The awkward thing about being related to somebody famous is that my life seems so ordinary by comparison. However, between you and me I'm kinda glad really. Flying around on apparatuses designed to sweep floors, battling with wizened old men who cast spells cannot be entirely safe, and to be honest is not really my cup of tea. I'll tell you what my cup of tea is though. It is in fact a cup of tea. China's finest black tea gently roasted over pine that leaves one feeling oh so refreshed and revitalised. There is something magic about having a cup of tea. It seems to fix any problem from bee stings, to broken arms. Nothing seems to come close to quenching one's thirst of an afternoon as a cup of tea.

Now don't get me wrong I am not one to discriminate, and I will drink the other tea, but only if its oolong. One has to draw a line in the sand somewhere. Although having said that the problem with drawing a line in the sand is that it doesn't last too long. My experience has shown me that the wind tends to blow it out of existence fairly quickly, usually before one has finished one's tea. Unless of course you are using wet sand. The difficulty there is that wet sand is usually found at the beach. The nuisance then of course is that one must contend with the tide, other beach goers trying to steal your sand for a sand castle or the fact the 99.9% of all beaches in the U.K. are stony beaches. Ones simply therefore cannot draw a distinct line anywhere. I mean who has ever heard of drawing a line in the stone. It just doesn't make sense.

But be that as it may. While so many have read about the daring exploits of my darling brother, not many have even heard of yours truly. I must admit though it does have its own rewards. Such as the time when I tried to start my own goat catching business.

One morning while imbibing a quiet cup of lapsang souchong at the Costa coffee in Godalming and pondering about where I could actually draw my line without it being blown or washed away, I overheard a conversation between two old dears in the booth next to me. They appeared to be talking about old people stuff so I wasn't really listening until the first said to the second. "And do you know what really gets my goat?" The second replied "No I don't! But do you know what gets mine?" Well that got me thinking if there is someone out there getting goats, it must be a goat catcher. An ideal business opportunity I thought. I mean there can't be too many people in Godalming in the goat catching business.

Wahoo 15 and my first real adventure. So off I set. With my trusted companion Herman Granger at my side, whom I subsequently contacted to help me on my journey of becoming the greatest goat catcher Godalming has ever seen.

If one is to become a goat catcher then one definitely

needs an assistant. Herman is the younger brother to my brother's best friend. I thought that he would be the best person to help me find these goats. Primarily it was because he had sufficient funds to keep me in tea. But not only that, he is my only friend. Everyone else had run off to be with my brother. So off we set full of enthusiasm and tea in search of these missing goats.

After about two hours of scouring the villages of Godalming and Farncombe, we stopped off at Natter for a quiet cup of nature's elixir to all ailments.

"Do you know what?" asked Herman, "I've got a good feeling about this."

"Me too" said I.

"I bet we end up getting lotsa goats," Herman continued. "Even though we haven't found any yet".

"I do hope so," I replied.

"But what we need to think about is what we are we going to do when we get all of these goats. I mean. Where are we going put them?" Herman stated.

"The thing is," I said, "There's only so much you can do with a goat".

"Like what?" Herman enquired.

"Well," I said pulling out my 101 things to do with a goat. "There's Goat curry. Goats head soup. Goat cheese. And a Goat bicycle rack."

"You're right. The fun is in the getting 'em I s'pose" said Herman. "I guess we could put 'em back." He said after a short pause.

"What do you mean?" I exclaimed, alarmed at the prospect of having to put the goat back after having just captured it.

"Well if someone's out there getting peoples goats,

imagine how cool it would be if there was someone out there giving them back to their rightful owner". Herman said rather thought provokingly

"That's it! We'll do that instead. I mean it can't be that hard identifying the original owners can it?" I said enthusiastically.
"No doubt they'll have collars with their names and addresses on, just like our dog Jumble," said Herman.

"Let's do it!" I exclaimed. So off we went filled with new vigor and enthusiasm in search if these lost goats. Soon we were intrepidly scouring the countryside scrambling over farmer's fences. Crossing the river Wey, then re-crossing the river. Looking in the old chamber of secrets that are the pillboxes on the river, and traipsing twice around Broadwater Lake.

We had to go around twice as half way around the first time Herman thought he'd seen a goat. Turns out it was just a Bergamasco Shepherd.

"What are the chances of seeing one of those here eh?" Herman muttered under his breath. "Coulda happened to anyone I guess," he mumbled somewhat disappointed.

I had to admit I was beginning to feel a little disappointed too. We'd been searching for quite some time and had not even so much as seen one goat, let alone goats plural.

After another couple of hours we arrived at Hectors at the Boathouse, somewhat exhausted and dejected from our travels around Godalming.

"This goat catching thing sure is thirsty work," remarked Herman.

How hard is it to catch a goat? It shouldn't be this

difficult, I thought. Surely not! However I was wrong. It was proving to be a little more difficult than I first anticipated.

"What I find just as perplexing," I started as I took a long sip of my tea, "and the answer to which has been as elusive to me as an elusive thing trying to elude me in a darkened room whist my eyes are blindfolded, is whether the Wombles of Wimbledon fame are common or in fact from Wimbledon common."

"I mean," I continued, "I have been to Wimbledon and indeed visited the common on numerous occasions and not once have I ever seen a Womble."

"Come to think of it. Neither have I," said Herman. "It may just mean however, that they're not that common after all," he continued.

"I think Mike Batt was lying to us all from the very beginning." I posited. "I believe that contrary to popular belief Wombles are in fact neither common nor are they from Wimbledon common."

"I agree," said Herman. "Although it could be that Wombles have incredibly short attention spans."

"What do you mean?" I asked.

"Well you know. It could be that they all walk along Wimbledon high street obviously not the common, and suddenly forget who they are, or that they live there."

"I still don't follow," I interjected quizzically. "Well if that is not so then why is it then that Mr. Batt thinks it is imperative that we all must remember, and by inference the humble Womble must remember that we, and they, are In fact Wombles."

"Or perhaps they are all live and well and driving in Guildford. I mean there seem to be an inordinate amount of Wombles on the road in Guildford, are there not?" I interjected again. Laughing at the thought of all these lost Wombles took us away from the disappointment of not finding a goat. When suddenly we heard the screeching of tyres. A man in a van was skidding on the road and came to an abrupt halt, narrowly missing a 4x4 Grange Drover that was now parked, well I say parked it was more like stationary in the middle of the road. There was a cacophony of noise as horns blared and drivers yelled at each other as they got out of the vehicles.

Everyone in the café was agog at the scene developing before our very eyes. Someone had decided that because they drove a large four x four Grange Drover that it meant that they had permission to park on the double yellow lines outside the café. Unfortunately no one had informed the driver behind. To exacerbate matters it appeared that the Grange Drover was also suffering from an electrical fault, or the driver of said vehicle had a broken arm, as we all heard that there was a complete failure from the Grange Drover to indicate that it wanted to pull over and stop there.

Things were getting rather heated for a bit. By this time most of the café had formed an orderly English queue outside so that they could watch the events unfold. Fortunately Constable Phil officer Stone arrived on the scene pretty quickly. It was just as well as the driver were reciting the Queensbury Rules, and describing each other's pedigree. However the Grange Drover driver somewhat reluctantly conceded that just because he owned a Grange Drover that it didn't give him permission to park on double yellow lines and that as painful as it was, he did not own the road. With a quick waving of Officer Stone's hand and with the threat of demerit points ringing in both driver's ears they were on their way pretty sharpish.

"You know what?" I asked Herman.

"What?" he replied.

"I think that the ordinary everyday Womble folk can be found driving on the roads of Godalming too."

"You're not wrong there," replied Herman.

"Hey look!" He almost shouted, pointing toward the van that was now some distance away. It was one of those fancy AZ Car Vans – a new hybrid something between a car and a van. It was not quite a car and not quite a van. On the back we were able to make out a picture of a large goat, with the words Prince Ces' Goat catching services emblazoned across the top. Inscribed underneath was by Order of the Phoenix County Council. It appeared that our luck had begun to turn for the better.

"Right! After we finish our tea we'll find a phone box and see if we can't get an address for Prince Ces' and his goat catching business."

"Hang on a minute," said Herman. "My tea is still hot it feels like this Goblet's on fire." It sounds somewhat familiar I thought but couldn't remember where I'd heard that before.

After waiting for what seemed like an eternity we departed and soon found a phone box half way down Catteshall Lane. After fighting with a trifid that had taken up residence in the box we managed to find the phone book. However much to our consternation the phone book had been torn to shreds. It appeared that the trifid was a hungry one and had devoured most of the book including all the yellow pages.

It was getting dark and the crickets were chirping by

the time we reached the phone box in the high street. All the shops had closed for the night except for 'Spoons, which was now starting to fill with the commuters on their way home from a hard day in London.

"You know what?" Herman asked as we finally located the address for the goat catching business.

"No! What's that?" I responded. "I bet you he isn't even a real prince."

"Its unlikely" I agreed.

"I will even go so far as to suggest that he isn't even a half of one?" continued Herman.

"You mean a half blood prince?" I asked. "You are probably right."

Fortunately lady luck was on our side once again and we discovered that the goat catchers were just behind the ambulance station back in Catteshall Lane, near the first phone box. We both looked at each other.

"Well we've come this far," Herman said. "It'd be pretty stupid if we didn't at least case the joint to see whether we can release Prince Ces' Prisoners."

I agreed that it seemed pretty foolish to give up now that we had come this far.

With renewed enthusiasm we headed off back toward Catteshall Lane and surprisingly we found the place very easily. It appeared to be abandoned, as one would expect at that time of night. I tried the door. It was locked. We walked around the yard but there was not a window open anywhere. The place seemed to be locked up tighter than spandex on a 350-pound woman.

"Well that buggers your plan to rule the universe then doesn't it?" said Herman somewhat despondently.

"Not quite yet," I retorted. "I'm not giving up that easily". With that I climbed up onto the roof of an adjacent building. It appeared to be an old Korean computer repair business. The sign on the door was fading but one could still make out Deeth Lee & Hal Lows computer repairs.

What happened next was pretty much a blur. I must have inadvertently triggered a silent alarm at some point. I recall finding window that although shut was not locked. I climbed in to have a closer look. I soon found the prisoner of AZ Car Van. He was standing on an old hessian sack munching on some old vegetables. I opened the back doors and let him out.

Just as I opened the door with the goat in hand who should arrive but Phil Officer Stone again.

"Ello! Ello! Ello!" said Officer Stone in his gruff voice. "What 'ave we 'ere then? A spot of breakin' an enterin' I'll be bound!"

"It's not what you think Officer Stone," I replied. "We are trying to return this goat to its rightful owner. You see someone really got this goat and we were merely attempting to return it," I tried in vain.

But he wasn't having any of it. He just kept on about the inappropriateness of taking other people's property, and climbing in windows that didn't belong to me. He also said that the goat catching business owned the goat. That the business made goat catchers – that they weren't goat catchers. Ethel was the goat that they used to demonstrate the equipment.

I don't know why he was getting so upset. I mean it was me who wanted to return it to its rightful owner. What I don't understand is that Goldilocks broke into and entered a house thereby committing burglary and trespass. She then proceeded to sample porridge, theft. She then committed criminal damage when she broke the chair. Finally she had the audacity to use one of the beds without colour of right or lawful excuse, which is conversion. The funny thing is that they wrote a book about her and they wanted to throw it at me. I don't think that's fair do you? Surely attempting to return a goat is nowhere near as bad as what Goldilocks did.

Again after reluctantly agreeing to shut down our goat catching venture Officer Stone agreed to talk to the owners who had now arrived. Fortunately the owners agreed not to press charges provided we promised never to go goat catching again. We did so pretty quickly. Officer Stone thought that the whole situation was so ridiculous that he couldn't believe I was related to somebody so famous. As the owners didn't want to press charges he let me off with a stern warning. Well what can I say but next time your goat is got; I think I'm just going to let it remain got.

Humphrey, Jeffrey and Godfrey

THE FURRICIOUS GANG MEET DONDUS

by Martyn Adams

Humphrey slapped his forehead in exasperation and wondered if today was going to be one of those difficult days.

It wasn't a very loud slap because teddy bears are pretty soft and furry. He'd been watching Jeffrey trying to learn to play the cello. Everyone, well everyone with an iota of sense anyhow, knows that a cello is a two teddy bear instrument. One bear would stand on a chair pressing the strings to make the notes on the fretboard while the second bear stood on the ground and sawed away at the strings with a bow.

But the results were usually poor at best because teddy bears, no matter how good they are at reading music, rarely agree on how fast to play it. Consequently multi-bear instruments usually result in one bear finishing before the others. In fact, the first to finish would often shout "I won!" and claim it as a victory.

It is for this reason that the record time for playing Chopin's Minute Waltz, or at least some of it, squarely lies with a teddy bear. The piano is a four bear instrument, one of them is required to press the pedals while the other three (when not squabbling over who should play which notes) share a very wide stool. The record sits with an Austrian by the name of Villhemina Pickelpaws Kleinbarr with a time of just over fourteen seconds. Of course she didn't have to play all the notes, her team mates achieved those some seconds later.

Teddy bears love classical music. But making it...? Not so good. This is why there are so few teddy bear orchestras. Besides, it takes great skill to be able to play an instrument, read the music, liaise with their instrumental partners, prepare a picnic and watch the conductor at the same time.

Moreover conductors of teddy bear orchestras, regardless of species, have to learn to cope with avoiding high speed ballistic crumbs - whether from biscuit eating trumpet players or sandwich eating trombonists. Let a teddy bear rest for just a few seconds and they'll soon find a snack to tuck into. This is not good if later on you are on the receiving end of a trumpet fanfare!

In fact a nearly indecipherable scribble on an original page of Verdi's Requiem, when translated, reads: 'For the sake of civility employ no teddy bears in the brass - unless the conductor and the audience are wearing armour!'

Another known problem is with teddy bears playing the timpani drums. Watching the bears jumping about on these wonderful instruments, as if they were trampolines, tends to distract the audience and very often the bears themselves. For instance playing Beethoven's Ninth will invariably end up with concussed bears flying all over the orchestra and getting stuck in the tubas.

So why was Jeffrey attempting to play the cello by himself? He had this theory that it really needed only one bear to play it. Consequently he had rigged up a cello to stand upside down. His paws would do the sawing with the bow while standing on one leg. The other leg would press the string to the neck to get the note.

It was not a pretty sound. And when the cello eventually fell on top of him - it was not a pretty sight. But at least the cello landed on something soft.

"It's time for our morning walk." Said Humphrey.

After Jeffrey had disentangled himself from the cello, and the bears had carefully replaced it back in its case and returned it to their secret store, they set off for their early morning constitutional along Godalming's Riverside Path.

Now these three bears, Humphrey, Jeffrey and Godfrey, live in a secret underground location very near the bandstand in Godalming's Philips Memorial Park. This park was named after Jack Philips, the hero who remained at his post, transmitting SOS messages, while the ocean liner RMS Titanic sunk. Sadly, he is also the twit that never delivered the latest iceberg warnings to the bridge. Nevertheless, in good old British tradition, his final act of heroism is the bit that's remembered and honoured, not his contribution to the actual sinking of it in the first place.

In Godalming's old cemetery there is also a memorial headstone dedicated to Philips but in the style of an iceberg. This confuses our bears because it seems to them that the ice-berg is also being honoured even though it's the homicidal object that killed him.

The bears thought of it this way, if you were run over by a car would you really want your final memorial to be the wheel that did the foul deed?

To teddy bears, humans – especially the adults – are a confusing lot.

The trio walked, sometimes skipped and sometimes ran along the path to the library. They played the game of 'It' and 'Hide and Seek' and as usual managed to dodge the very, very early morning joggers – which was all part of the fun. On their way back they visited their friend the Tree Woof who gave them some beetfruit to take home. All this time Humphrey kept a wary eye out for alligators for, although his friends kept telling him there weren't any in Surrey, Humphrey informed them that one had once chased him up a tree along this very same path.

They were soon safely back at their secret bear lair when Godfrey let out a little cry.

"I've losted my beetfruit!"

"Where did you lost… I mean, lose it?"

"On the path."

"Quickly then, nip out and get it."

So Godfrey nipped out and ran down the path until he saw his little bag. He grabbed it, opened it and tested to see if the contents tasted like they looked. They did, so he started wandering back.

A rustle and a little splashing from the bushes by the river and Godfrey froze, eyes as wide as small dinner plates. Ahead of him, slowly rising from the river, was a bright green but very smooth head on a long slender neck. It was chomping on grass. It looked at him and winked.

"Uhm…" Said Godfrey.

The head rose even higher and smiled while at the same time continuing to chew.

"Uhm…" Said Godfrey, certain he knew what he wanted to say but too terrified to say it.

The head dropped behind the bushes again and Godfrey waited, or more accurately his legs simply refused to run. Then the monster re-appeared chewing more grass. It slowly looked around.

Still terrified, but now not so petrified, Godfrey squeaked the first thing that came to mind.

"Hello?"

The creature's head turned and it looked down at the little bear. It smiled again, swallowed and said in a very,

very deep voice, "Hello."

Godfrey, still frightened but now slightly less terrified squeaked.

"My name is Godfrey."

"My name is Dondus." boomed the monster.

"Uhm, are you a... a... a allin-gator?"

"No. I'm a dopacus."

"D-do you eat t-teddy bears?"

"No. I'm a vegan."

Godfrey weighed the two previous answers and was still not quite happy.

"I thought you said you were a donkey?"

"No. I am a dopacus."

"Oh."

"I am also a vegan. I only eat grass. I do not eat teddy bears." He smiled again.

"Oh." Godfrey was feeling a lot more confident now. Still frightened, but not nearly as much as before he regarded the animal's smooth green skin. "Why don't you have any hair?"

The monster thought for a moment. "So it doesn't get wet?"

Godfrey felt reassured at that. To him that seemed like a logical answer.

"I've got fur."

"You are a very observant little bear." Remarked Dondus.

"Do you know Woof?"

"I know many ways of making a noise."

Godfrey frowned, confused.

"No. I mean, do you know Woof who lives in the Beetfruit Tree?"

"Oh yes. We are great friends. Sometimes I give him river rides."

"River rides? What's a River Ride?"

"Let me show you." Said the dopacus and his head zoomed toward the little bear...

"Jeffrey! Have you seen Godfrey?" Humphrey was in the kitchen cleaning the clockwork dishwasher with a damp rag and wondering why nobody had thought to invent a dishwasher-washer. He then idly mused that, if there was such a thing then someone might have to invent something to clean the little rubber grommets that go in them – and the person that cleaned *that* machine would be called a dishwasher-washer-washer-washer washer.

Jeffrey ran into the kitchen wielding a bottle of fizzy drink in his paws.

"Look Humphrey! See what happens when I do this!" He put his thumb over the top and then shook the bottle up and down as vigorously as he could.

"Stop! Don't you dare spray that all over my nice clean kitchen. *You* will have to clean it up if you do!" He frowned to make his point. "Have you seen Godfrey? He was supposed to be back ten minutes ago." He took his little pink floral pinny off.

Jeffrey stopped and shook his head "Godfrey? I don't know."

"I'd better get out there and see what's happened to

him. You stay here and don't you *dare* make a mess!"
Humphrey stared threateningly at Jeffrey then climbed up
to the front door to let himself out. Before he stepped
outside he stopped and turned to check that his message
had got through.

Jeffrey was looking down at the fizzing bottle very
worried that it could pop at any moment and make a mess.
His thumb couldn't contain the building pressure for long.
That would be bad. Very bad.

Without a moment's hesitation, or thought, he made a
decision and stuck the neck in his mouth and let his thumb
off the top. There was a 'POOMPH' sound and his arms
and legs snapped open, his cheeks distended, his ears went
rigid and his eyes almost popped out of his head – but he
valiantly kept his mouth closed around the neck of the
bottle. The (very) fizzy drink didn't make a mess.

Humphrey winced.

After a few moments the high pressure gasses
eventually found an exit point and Jeffrey started to make
a very long, loud, high-pitched screeching sound. His body
pivoted on the tip of his left leg as the thrust from
escaping gasses lifted him slightly off the floor. His puffed
out cheeks turned red with embarrassment as he caught
sight of Humphrey staring back at him with complete and
utter disbelief – and the high-pitch noise changed to a sort
of flubberling sound and gradually got lower and lower,
and louder and louder, and ruder and ruder.

Humphrey slapped his forehead in exasperation. Today
was turning out to be one of those days. He turned and
left Jeffrey to sort himself out. He had to find Godfrey.
Then he heard Godfrey's squeaky voice from the far side
of the reeds.

"Wheeeee! Faster Dondus, faster!"

He peered through the greenery at the river and to his

amazement saw Godfrey grinning wildly, paws held out high and whizzing along the river at an altitude of close to nothing above the river. Humphrey's eyes nearly popped. How could Godfrey be flying at all? Let alone while sitting on his bottom just a centimetre or so above the river's surface? Surely it wasn't aerodynamic...

Then the little bear slowed and stopped and Humphrey's eyes nearly popped again as Godfrey rose out of the water atop a large green grinning head.

"Godfrey... ?"

"Hullo Humph! I'm flying! Wheeeee!"

"So I see. It's time to come indoors now. People will be about soon."

"Sorry Dondus. I've got to go now. Can you put me down?"

The big head, on top of a long neck, moved forward and down and Godfrey elegantly stepped on to the riverside path beside Humphrey.

"Bye bye Dondus." Godfrey waved. "Thank you for the river ride."

The green head winked at him and then smiled back at the two bears before disappearing under the surface of the river.

"Who... ? What... ? Was... ? Was what... ? Who was that?"

"That was Dondus. He's a donkey. He lives in the river and eats grass. He's wet but he doesn't have fur to get wet with."

Humphrey tried to recall if there were any long-necked river-dwelling green donkey breeds living in Surrey.

"He's not Scottish is he? I understand that the Loch

Ness monster hasn't been spotted for a while."

"No. Dondus doesn't have spots. He's green." Godfrey replied. At that moment a car drove over the bridge so Humphrey grabbed Godfrey by an ear and they made a dash for their secret entrance. They mustn't be spotted by people.

They just got inside their secret bear lair when Godfrey noticed Jeffrey in the middle of the lounge. Jeffrey was still rigid, arms outstretched and cheeks puffed out, slowly rotating on his left tip-toes like a well inflated ballet-dancing balloon. The bottle was still poking out of his mouth. Jeffrey's eyes were now crossed and he was starting to turn purple with the effort of holding his breath while at the same time holding in the fizzy gasses in his body – and failing.

But it was the rude noises that set Godfrey into hysterics of laughter. Humphrey watched bemused as Godfrey fell over giggling and holding his sides. He started to roll about on the carpet.

Humphrey sighed, crossed his arms and leaned against the wall to wait and see what happened next.

It was a full three minutes later before Jeffrey started to deflate and managed to stand upright properly. Godfrey had been giggling so much now his sides hurt and his giggles had become interspersed with "Ha ha ha - Ow! Ha ha - Ow! Ha mhmh – Ow! Ow! Ow! Ha - It hurts!" And other various little whimpering noises.

Two minutes later Jeffrey had extracted the – now empty – bottle of fizzy drink from his mouth with a pop and a king-sized belch – which blew him backwards into the wall. He was dazed but thankful that it was all over.

Godfrey was in tears. It was difficult to tell if they were tears of laughter of tears of pain. Or both. His sides still hurt.

When he calmed down Humphrey asked him a question.

"Okay. Now the fun is over. Godfrey can you tell me more about the green monster?"

Godfrey looked up at Humphrey with an insane grinning grimace and managed...

"Oooh... Who? My sides hurt."

"Dondus. The bald-green-donkey-in-river-type-thing. Godalming's answer to Loch Ness. What can you tell me about him?"

"Who?" Godfrey looked genuinely puzzled. "Oooh... My sides hurt." He had forgotten all about his river ride – at least for the moment. Maybe he'd remember later.

Humphrey sighed, bent down and cuddled little Godfrey, consoling him.

Jeffrey burped again. This time a more civilised (if a burp can ever be civilised) teddy-bear burp. But it was enough to set off Godfrey howling with laughter / pain again.

Jeffrey, pleased with his humorous effect on the little bear, ran to the bottle rack to fetch another bottle of fizzy drink.

Humphrey slapped his forehead in exasperation. Today *was already* one of those difficult days.

Jack Phillips, the Titanic's radio officer, was born in Farncombe and the Phillips Memorial was constructed by public subscription in 1913 to commemorate his bravery at sea. The memorial is the largest in the country to commemorate a single member of crew...

THE BLANK PAGE

By Stefan Kuegler, Martyn Adams, Elif Tyson & Ian Honeysett

I sit and think about what to write.

I look out the window as the train moves along towards its destination. A destination that I'm not sure I want to reach. I see a tree speed by and know that I wish we were traveling in the reverse direction.

I knew that this day would come. I had been doing everything to put it off but finally I couldn't put it off any longer. I was still taking the easy way out. Although at this point it didn't seem like an easy way. The page in front of me refused to be filled with words. It stayed blank to spite me. The fear and worry that have consumed me for the past few days (weeks really) continue to stay my hand.

I leaned back, trying to find a restful position but nothing seems to be comfortable. First class it might be on the ticket – the blue seats matched my mood. I continue to struggle to find a comfortable position for my body as my mind also struggles with the thoughts that consume it. Neither body nor mind are at peace.

The words still don't come. I wanted to make it personal. I could have written an email but that would have been cowardly. After what I had done, I certainly wasn't cowardly.

I look out the window seeking inspiration. Fields stretch into the distance as I watch the suburban life as it rushes around. I watch from my vantage point on the speeding train. I feel isolated in my seat removed from the demands of the needs of modern man. For a moment I can find peace and rest while I enjoy the journey. I am not in that race. The corner of my eye spies the blank page. I know I am in a race of a different kind.

The train slows. A station. I see the name. The panic rises. The blank page in front of me is imploring me to write something. Anything. But how do you write about what I have done. How can say what I feel? How can I convey what needs to be said.

The station appears. I watch as the few people get on and off the train. I tried to smile as they sit nearby but I'm sure it is more a grimace. How can they know the pain I feel? The train starts to move again.

"Godalming, next stop. Your next stop is Godalming."

The announcement has sealed my fate. I pick up the pen determined to write something. It shouldn't be that difficult but the frustration and anxiety now, of the blank page, has reached epic proportions.

I can't see the words for the white space.

I laugh, trying to ease my tension. It is forced and I feel no better. It ends up being a cough. People look at me strangely.

I wonder how my lack of words will be received. Am I making too much of it? Does it matter what I write? Will they even read it? Once they notice the hand-writing they will see it was from me. Will they even care? Can they comprehend what I had to do?

The train slows again. Godalming already. I freeze. What if I just stay in my seat? Stay on to Haslemere. Keep on going forever. Continue to hide. To run. Shall I be honest and tell all or let them continue to think what they may? Does it matter? I know for a change it matters to me. This is one thing that I cannot let go. I have lived my whole life with deceptions. For once it worked but now I know I have to make it right.

The doors are about to close. A bitter taste fills my mouth. I leap up from my seat and get off – just in time. The guard gives me a scornful look. He blows the whistle and the train moves off. The die is cast.

I breathe deeply. I remember the town. Friendships made. Friendships broken. A lifetime ago since I had been back. I knew that this would be my last visit. I couldn't stay. The memories would be too painful.

"Alex – not seen you for a while!" I turn around and there is Rory or is it Rolf? How did he recognise me? Any notion I had of walking to the other side and catching the train the other way were dashed. My visit would eventually reach the right ears and then more questions would follow.

"Look, old chap, can I give you a lift? The car's just down in the carpark." Rory points out the station doors. "I was lucky to get a space today, I can tell you. Some days…"

"Sorry," I mumble, "but I've an urgent appointment. Some other time perhaps."

"Have you indeed?" Rory pauses for a moment. I wonder what he is thinking. Maybe he sees the terror that I am feeling. Whatever he thinks, he shrugs and waves, leaving me in my misery. I put my head down, and set off towards the town. I need to think! I need to write something. I'll have a half pint at The Star, my favourite pub. I can sit in the garden at the back and write that letter. Yes, that's a great idea.

Ten minutes later I'm sat there with my pint – a half seemed inadequate for what I have to do. And I won't leave here till it's written. It's a nice sunny evening and not too busy. No one I know so it's as perfect as it's going to get.

I've got to be honest, after all. Mostly with myself. I need to explain myself. I need to write the letter for myself as much as for others. That ridiculous allegation. I mean, how could anyone believe there was an iota of truth to it? Well, okay, maybe an iota but no more than that. How could I tell them the truth? How could I say? I had promised. For once in my life I had kept it. For once I believed what I was doing.

I won't dismiss what I had done in the past. I mean we all make mistakes. I looked at the empty glass in front of me. I look at the page. There are words. Or was I dreaming? I had been written while thinking and some of my thoughts had been etched on the page.

I've made a start.

Another pint and I might finish it. It's getting quite busy in here now and there are several people at the bar. I go to the bar - it takes ten minutes to get served and then some klutz jolts my arm and I spill some of my beer over his girlfriend's pretty blue dress. I mumble an apology though it really should be him apologising. She makes an extremely un-ladylike comment. Very coarse. I think about saying something but stop myself. In the past I would have been outside or inside for that matter taking matters in hand.

Not today. I need to be gone. I make my way back to my table when I see, to my horror, that someone is sitting in my place! I panic. I'd left the page on the table. The paper with my first words all day in my beautifully legible handwriting, is gone!

What to do?

"Excuse me. Did you see a page here? I left it when I went to the bar." The woman sitting there looks up and then around, shrugs. Back to her phone. It was a token look, nothing more. Did I expect anything else? I look down and see the page on the ground.

I place the pint on the table and lean down. I pull the page off the floor. A little crumpled but at least I can make out the words.

I mumble something. She doesn't even look up. I pick up my pint and search for another seat. I nearly fall into my new seat. I look around. Still no one I know. I place the page on the table in front of me. I have a drink of the pint to calm myself. I was feeling less panicked. I look over the words. They are ramblings. I know what I mean and what I'm trying to say but no one else will. I stare so hard now I can even see the details of the texture in the paper almost looking back to me.

Maybe they were right in their comments. The doubts return. I can't blame anybody and I also need to forgive myself. I made the decision. If I manage to make peace with myself then possibly I can heal my other relationships. It would take time. The letter that I need to write would help. At the moment it is not helping anyone.

I loved this place and I loved Godalming. I stop as a flood of memories come back. Of this place and of things in the town. It wouldn't have changed much. I think of the days I used to happily live here - just up the Frith Hill. Used to watch the frost rising on the Lammas Land and the river and even could see the part of the railway. Idyllic spot for some and I took it for granted. Now, unless some miracle happens I will never see it again.

It would be much more suitable if I put all my thoughts on the paper then go through them to understand and make my point. This will not be an apology, this will be the truth. I can leave them to think what they will. I will know I acted the way I did for the right reason.

How much do they know? How much have they guessed? How much will they believe? When was it? It was

Friday afternoon over a year ago now. That long ago already. Just the start of a long weekend. Bank holiday. That was why we did it.

I finish my beer as the memories continue thick and fast. Now I am staring to my empty glass. The tears don't start but somehow I would welcome them. Should I have another? I place my empty glass in front of me. I move quickly to get another – having convinced myself that I didn't need it. It would be the last. At least for today.

Cradling my pint as if it was delicate piece of china, I managed to dodge the milling clientele back to my place. No one had taken it this time. Relief – until that half formed memory returned again. Damn it! I tried blotting it out but the trying only made things worse.

In the end I leaned back, took a long drink of the pint. The memories needed to come, perhaps they would help me form the words. I could see the faces - the people that needed to be told. People I loved. Had loved. Still loved in a way.

I closed my eyes and heard the soothing voice of the therapist. What was her name now? Greta? Yes. That was it. 'Greater Greta' was my nickname for her. I wondered how old she was, it was difficult to remember. She liked to wear a droopy brown wool cardigan and ridiculously long ear rings, with silver bangles on her wrists that shone and flashed with every slight movement she made. She reminded more of a fortune teller rather than a psychiatrist. She was very non-medical for one supposedly in the healing profession. She smiled a lot and quite often it seemed genuine.

It had been one session but I remember it. I had to talk to someone. I hadn't said everything but enough so she could help. Enough so I could feel some relief. She had helped. The lies had started so far back. I wished I could speak to her now.

A group of friends out together across from me laugh.
Loud enough to jolt me from my memories and back to
my page. I squinted at the trio laughing and nudging at
each other. I could hear their words, something about last
night's party, but that wasn't of interest to me. Three
young men. One in particular catches me, tugs at a
memory. It was his eyes. They are the same. The same
colour. The same sorrow. Just like Zurich.

I look down at the paper and pen again. Was this
helping? Suddenly I know what to write. The words flow. I
look at the young man again – the words flow from
somewhere in the heart, somewhere from the depths of
my very soul. I write something that would make them
understand, make them think better of me. I needed to do
this.

I remember Zurich. Remember the last words that
were spoken to me; "I will die quietly. Don't think no-one
loves you. I do. I will think good of you. You helped. I
thank you. I will die quietly..."

Her eyes showed happiness. No struggle. Acceptance. I
had helped. The pain was gone. Her face was smooth. The
years of pain were gone. I had silenced it. No one else had.
No one else had the courage. Even as her last futile
breathe became feeble and then finally, she was still. And I
remember feeling, not regret, not horror, but satisfaction.
Satisfaction at a job well done. I wonder now how I could
think that way.

I can live in the past as much as I want but it will
change nothing. There is a future out there and I want to
be part of it. I need to start something. I curse the fool
that made me lose my ideas but I start to calm myself to
re-write what I had done.

Now that I was really thinking about it, the words
came. The difficulty lay in my head, trying, as usual to
come up with the right words. There were no words that

were going to make this any better. I had suffered and others will too. I could only say the truth. I could only speak what I felt.

I take a breath and look at the page in front of me, crumpled though it may be, it had the words that I wanted to say. I picked up my drink and paused. I had already had a few too many trying to get the courage up to write these few words. I needed my wits about me now. The difficult part was still to come.

As much as the words had been the hard part, there was also relief at writing them. Relief flowed through my veins and now I could move onto what was next. For next was the delivery, I knew the place and had pictured it in my mind ever since I knew that I had to do this. My feet would lead me. I didn't need to look.

I hadn't thought it would be so hard coming back to Godalming. The sights and sounds reminding me of a time when I was happier, unburdened. Now the weight of guilt and betrayal hung on me.

I look around the Star. I pick up my glass for the last time. It was time to go. I could stay but then the risk was of one drink too many of letting my emotions take over. I couldn't let that happen today. Too much was contained. Held in suspense. I picked up my letter, pulling as I did an envelope from my jacket pocket. I stuck the letter inside and then sealed it.

I stepped out onto the footpath, placed the letter back inside my jacket.

"Alex?"

I turn, checking out who had called my name but also who else was in the street. It was deserted although there was likely to be people walking along it soon. The trains arrived regularly at Godalming and those who got off at the station a steady traffic moved up Church Street looking for the main part of town. What could I do?

"Yeah, Steve, isn't it?"

"It's been, what, five years?"

"At least." A quick glance tells me that still no one is around. I take a step away from the pub, hoping that the movement would be in the opposite direction to Steve. I now didn't have time for this. And, although I could remember his name, I couldn't quite recall why. He was familiar but I wasn't sure the reason.

"Time for a half?"

I reply, with what sounds to me like a slight slurring or my words, that I've just left the pub. He nods. There seems a nature silence, indicating a parting of ways.

"Actually, it's odd bumping into you like this. Why are you back?" His mood has changed. At first it had been friendly. I could sense an undercurrent of hostility. What should I say? I just wanted to deliver my letter and go. I was now desperate to leave.

"This and that." I didn't want to engage. I was hoping he would just leave me.

"I heard about you last time you were here."

Here it comes. I had braced myself for this sort of reaction if I spotted someone who would know me.

"You piece of shit. I should flatten you now."

I held up my hands. "You don't understand."

"Like hell. I should ring the police."

"Don't." I look around, frantic, wondering how I can get out of this. I need to move. I turn back to Steve. I see his fist moving fast. The landscape tilts.

I black out.

When I woke, still feeling blurry, I was in a chair. My nose ached and I could feel a light pressure, or maybe it was bruising, on my cheek. I try to raise my hand but can't. It takes a moment to realise that I am tied to the chair. I was restrained. Each arm and each leg was tied to a part of the chair. I try to stand.

"I wouldn't."

I looked around. He is standing there, watching. What is he doing?

I am about to shout out something, something unoriginal like 'Help!' or 'Untie me!' I get angry. Just when I'd finally got the courage I feel thwarted. This wasn't the way it was supposed to happen. I sigh. Nothing I can say or do will change it. I know that.

"Why are you doing this?"

"I'm not doing it for me."

The look of horror makes him laugh.

"What did you do?"

"You'll see." Steve picks up my jacket which he had taken off me. He feels the letter, stops and looks for it.

"What's this?"

I lay back, close my eyes and try to relax. What should I say? I hear the rip and open my eyes.

"Don't. Please."

My pleas fall on deaf ears. He tears it open.

"A letter? Email not good enough?"

I stay silent. He pulls it out and reads it.

I waited. There was nothing else to do. I wondered

what I should expect. Would he believe it? Would he say something? Would it all be alright?

"What is this?"

Knock knock. Steve turned towards me. "How much of it was true?" There was some disbelief in his voice. He obviously didn't think it could be.

Knock knock.

"Does it matter?"

Steve left. I sat in anguish for a few minutes as I waited.

He returned but this time the letter wasn't in his hand. It was in the hand of his visitor. I recognised her. How could I not? She was my sister, Eva. I hadn't seen her for nearly year. I see the pain there. The betrayal. All the things that I had built into the image of her. The face I would see.

She thrust the letter out in front of her. "Is this true?"

"For once, I can say it is. I don't know whether you believe me. I hope you do but I can understand if you don't. Or if you don't want to."

Eva sat down in the chair opposite. He re-read the letter or at least some parts of it.

"When?"

"Two year ago."

"She never told me."

"She didn't want to worry you." I didn't know the real reason but I assumed it was something like that. Our mother never worried about how I felt. Eva was the special one. I was the failure until last year. Until the last.

"How could you?"

"She asked. She was in constant pain."

"Where?"

"Zurich."

She sat in silence for a moment longer. She looked up at Steve, as if finally realising the situation. "Why is he tied to the chair?"

Steve moved to untie me. "I didn't want him leaving before you got here."

The cords came off and my hands and legs burned. I rubbed my wrists.

"I'm sorry."

"Where is she?"

"On my shelf. You can have her if you want." I stopped. What had I just said? "I'm sorry."

"Did she suffer?"

He half-smiled. "Not at the end. She was in peace. She wanted it. The pain had been too much for her. She hid it for too many months. She couldn't anymore. She wanted peace."

"But why just go? I don't understand."

"She wanted to die her own way."

"Did she leave anything? A note? A letter?" Eva said, as she held out the letter to me.

"I have a tape. Her final words and a message for you."

"Where?"

"In my pocket. My jacket pocket." Steve thrust out my jacket to me as if it was suddenly dangerous. I grabbed it and pulled the tape from the pocket. I looked at it, knowing that it would probably not answer the questions in Eva's head.

"I'm sorry." I said again. It had more meaning this time.

"I'm glad you were with her. I miss her."

Finally I could grieve. I could release the tears that had not flowed before. With my sister, the pain of the loss of our mother could be endured. I had sat with her when she had an assisted death in a foreign country and now I could finally admit that I was not so strong. I missed her too. But at least I could see the relief in her face as she passed. No more pain. No more suffering.

ABOUT THE AUTHORS

Stefan Kuegler

Stefan is a new author, writing both young adult and fantasy fiction books. He is a coach and has written one life management book to help in his work. Stefan has also started a property investment business (www.bluemountainsproperty.com) to allow him to have further time for writing.

Stefan has spent the last ten years writing for pleasure and felt it was time to get serious with it. He is currently working on a three volume fantasy epic while trying to manage chaos in Godalming, Surrey.

Ian Honeysett

After varied careers in Teaching (history & politics), Careers, Training & Human Resources, Ian decided to retire. Married to Jan, they have 3 children who live as far away as Coulsdon, New Zealand & Witley. For 16 years he was a School Governor but has also now retired from that.

So he currently devotes himself to writing (having co-written crime novels set in the French Revolution : http://goo.gl/Jecc7D), painting, editing (a magazine for laryngectomees), military history, quizzes (he runs a U3A Quiz group), St Edmund's Parish work & playing the ukulele. So he's still quite busy. He also quite likes to travel & has visited China, New Zealand, Canada & Alaska in recent years. He has an interesting collection of waistcoats.

Martyn Adams

Martyn lives and works in Godalming. He is a lightly bearded, 1950s vintage, software development manager at a local financial services company. Apart from writing his other main hobby is composing songs and playing them to select groups.

When he gets philosophical he likes to muse on the fact that we *all* live together on the crust of a single ball of molten rock while it whizzes round and around a deadly nuclear fireball. Some of us look up into the sky and hope that there's nothing out there that that will bump into us. Meanwhile we are poisoning our home and squabbling amongst ourselves for reasons that he *completely* fails to understand.

Elif Tyson

Elif enjoys living and working in Godalming. She is not a 'writer' as such but joined the group with intention of finishing her late husband's novel. Her only contribution to 'From a Couch in the Kings Arms' has been several paragraphs on the joint story … 'A Blank Page'. And going forward, she is hoping to fill hers.

Heather Wright

Heather has lived in the Godalming area since 1969. She has two sons who were educated locally and was herself a head teacher in Guildford for 23 years. Writing is her hobby and she has written family stories for her grandchildren mainly because their grandfather died before they were born and she wanted them to have some fun stories about him and their house which was their great adventure.

Judy Coleman

Judy's love of writing began at the age of eight and her work was selected to be read on Hugh Weldon's BBC Children's Hour. During the many years she lived in Cumbria, she exhibited paintings as a trained artist. Again her stories and poems were included in Radio Cumbria broadcasts and she wrote articles on Cumbrian artists for a magazine and local newspapers. Moving to Godalming to be near her family she became 'Artist in Residence' at Winkworth Arboretum for a year. Recently she joined a writing workshop to return to her love of words.

Ron Macdonald

Ron Macdonald born in Aberdeen, Scotland moved to Heston, Middlesex in 1937 then moved to Canada in August 1946 where he learned to fly at 17 in 1947. During his career he was a mechanic, inspector, test pilot & TCA Air Canada pilot for over 38 years with total flying hours of 24,800 hours. He has lived in Thursley, Godalming for 24 years & is a member of PETS (Players of Elstead Theatrical Society) and Brooklands Museum.

James Tong

James Tong is a Screenwriter, Will Writer, Property Investor, husband, father, karate student, actor and all round nice guy, who has lived and worked in Godalming since 2010. After immigrating to the UK from New Zealand in 2009 James worked as a Lawyer for a firm in Guildford that specializes in child protection and family law. In 2013 James completed a screen-writing course at a London University, so after being made redundant in 2014, James commenced his writing career. You can usually spot him dropping his children off at school in his distinctive hat or shorts.

Christine Butler

Christine Butler moved to Witley, just south of Godalming, in September 1980. At that time she and her husband Len had an old four-berth fibreglass Callumcraft cruiser moored on the River Wey at Farncombe Boathouse. She worked in Farnham, as a Personal Taxation Assistant in a bank, for many years. When she was made redundant in 2001 she joined a firm of accountants in Godalming, thus finishing her working life in the same town as it started in 1962. She didn't enjoy her first job at British Drug Houses' laboratories in Godalming and left after a few months.

Her main hobbies are family history and writing. When she retired in 2005 she took the opportunity to join an Adult Education Creative Writing course to learn about writing fiction rather than just articles for canal society and family history journals. Only once has she been paid for an article, so far. That was a piece for Evergreen Magazine about children's author Monica Edwards who lived in Thursley.

Printed in Great Britain
by Amazon